CANDACE GOLD'S
BOOK OF SHORTS
VOLUME TWO

A MOST HORRIFIC CRIME
By Candace Gold

I had gotten out of the hospital on Tuesday. The surgeon had removed another malignant tumor from my stomach. Between the treatments and the surgery, I felt as if I was caught in a revolving door, in and out of hospitals. I knew I was lucky to be alive. I fought to stay alive because I knew my family needed me, especially Robin, my baby daughter. My husband Ralph took care of her while I was away. Luckily, he was able to because he worked from the house.

I thought things were going to be all right. I had survived another surgery and the doctors felt they got the entire tumor. I guess in the long-range scheme of things, I had bought some more time and began to breathe a little easier until the day that the police showed up at my door.

Ralph was out. He had left an hour or so before to meet a client. Robin was napping so I took advantage of the quiet and was resting myself until the loud knocking on the front door woke me.

I opened the door to discover two men standing there. The taller man asked, "Mrs. Canby?"

"Ye...yes?"

"I'm Detective O'Brien and this is Detective Sills." Both men flashed their gold shields at me. "May we come in?"

I opened the door and led them into the living room.

"Is Mr. Canby at home?"

"No," I said hearing the quiver in my voice. Why were the police here? I was worried that Ralph might have done something unscrupulous like a shady business deal and had gotten caught. I was afraid I might say something incriminating.

"Do you expect him soon or is there a number you can reach him at?"

"I'll go see if his appointment book is in his office," I said, practically fleeing from the room.

I collapsed into Ralph's oversized leather chair. His appointment book wasn't on his desk or in his top drawer where he sometimes kept it.

When I returned to the living room Detective Sills was studying the family pictures, while Detective O'Brien was finishing a phone call on his cell phone.

"Did you find the appointment book?" asked Detective O'Brien?

I shook my head. "He must have taken it with him."

"Did he happen to mention the name or address of the client he was meeting?"

"No. Please, tell me what this is all about?"

"We need to ask him some questions," Detective Sills explained.

The way he looked at me made me feel uncomfortable as if he was scrutinizing me. *Why? How could I be involved?* He lifted a picture of Robin off an end table. "Is this your little girl?"

"Yes. Her name is Robin."

"She's beautiful. How old is she?"

"Going to be four next month. Do you have children?"

"Yes. Twin girls. They're twelve years old."

Detective O'Brien's cell phone rang. He walked out of the room to talk. Detective Sills pointed to another picture. "Is this your husband?"

"Yes, that's Ralph."

He nodded. "You married long?"

"Five years."

The other detective returned. "We're going to wait for your husband to return. Go about whatever you were doing and forget we're here."

He had to be kidding when he said that. How in the world was I to feel comfortable with two policemen sitting in my living room waiting to question and maybe arrest my unsuspecting husband when he returned home? And I had no way to warn him of what was in store for him.

"Would you care for something to drink?"

"No, we're fine," Detective O'Brien, said, speaking for both of them.

The front door opened. Ralph walked into the living room. "Who are you and what are you doing in my house?"

"Ralph! These men are policemen."

"They can speak for themselves, Jane."

"Ralph Canby?" Detective O'Brien asked.

"Yes. Were you expecting someone else? My wife isn't into that kind of business."

I was mortified when he said that, even though I realized it was out of anger. But why should he be angry—unless he knew why they were here or had something to hide.

"We have a warrant for your arrest and seizure of all your computer hardware and software," Detective Sills replied, ignoring Ralph's small outburst.

"On what grounds?"

Detective Sills stated, "Sexual abuse of a minor and child pornography. And endangering the welfare of your own child, for starters."

I heard myself gasp and covered my face with my hands. There was no way in the world that my husband could be capable of doing such terrible things. And with *our* baby? This was totally insane. Yet, I had a terrible feeling in the pit of my stomach that my entire world was going to be turned inside out.

"You're crazy!" Ralph practically screamed. "I'll have your badges for false arrest."

Detective O'Brien walked behind Ralph. "Slowly put your hands behind your back." He handcuffed him as he read him his rights. As he was doing this, Detective Sills had walked to the door and opened it to a group of men. They walked in wearing gloves.

"Tell your goons to be careful with that equipment. It's all expensive stuff," Ralph demanded.

"I'm certain it is," Detective O'Brien replied.

"Jane, call Ron Liebman. Tell him to meet me at the police station and get me out."

Nearly in shock with a new crop of tears taking residence in my eyes, I watched the parade of people leave my house with Ralph handcuffed in the lead. I roused myself into action and went to call our lawyer. He was at court, so I left a message for him to call as soon as possible.

There was a knock at the door. It was the two detectives again. I let them back in wondering why they hadn't accompanied Ralph to the police station. What could they have forgotten?

"Sorry to barge back in on you like this, Mrs. Canby, but we've got to ask you some important questions," Detective Sills explained.

"There's nothing I can tell you."

"I'm sure there is."

I shook my head no. "I can't believe any of this. Ralph is a good husband and a good father. I don't know what I would have done without him."

"In what way?" Detective O'Brien asked.

"I have stomach cancer. I've been in and out of hospitals. It's hard to take care of a child when you can hardly care for yourself."

"We understand. So basically, the sole care of your child fell upon your husband's shoulders?"

I bit my lower lip and nodded. Whenever I thought about that I felt like less of a mother. "But he wouldn't..."

"Wouldn't what?"

"Wouldn't hurt Robin in any way. He's so gentle with her..."

"Did he want to have a child?"

"More than anything. He was so excited when I told him that I had become pregnant. And when I found out it was a little girl, he seemed to be beside himself with joy."

The two men looked at each other when I said that. I felt as if I had hurt Ralph by saying the wrong thing. I wanted to run away. Therefore, when I heard Robin stirring, I nearly ran inside to check on her.

Seeing her golden curls and apple cheeks always brought a smile to my face. She was my little angel. Had Ralph hurt her in any way?

She saw me enter her room and held her little hands out. I sat down on her bed and held her to me. I looked at her she seemed the same, but was she different? How would I know? Being sick and away from her a great deal, was I a competent judge? What kind of mother did that make me? I was supposed to protect her from harm.

Robin and I went into the living room. The detectives smiled when they saw her. She always made people smile. That's the kind of child she was.

"Hello, Robin," Detective Sills said.

Robin giggled.

"She's beautiful," the detective added.

"Robin's my little angel. How could you accuse Ralph of such a horrific crime?"

"It's not something we contrived from the air, Mrs. Canby," Detective O'Brien stated. "Your husband offered to swap Robin with other men who had young daughters. One of the men who claimed to have a nine-year-old daughter was actually an undercover detective."

I gasped. How could this be so? Maybe it's all a colossal mistake.

"None of that can be true."

"Are you so sure?" Detective Sills asked.

"Your husband bragged on the internet how he'd been training your daughter since she was three months old. There are pictures of him with the child doing unspeakable things," Detective O'Brien added.

"Have you seen those terrible pictures?"

"Not yet. The ones that the undercover detective downloaded are in the possession of the D.A."

"Then the man *could* be mistaken."

"No, I'm afraid not."

"There's got to be an explanation. My husband is a *good* father."

"I understand your reluctance to accept any of this," Detective Sills added, "but the evidence speaks for itself."

"We find no pleasure in deplorable cases like these," Detective O'Brien said. "Children are too precious to be treated like sex toys."

The detectives stayed and questioned me a little longer. I had all but tuned them out. How could I believe that Ralph could have done such terrible things to the child he loved? And wouldn't Robin cry when he went near her? No. My husband was not a pedophile. He would never touch Robin the way he touched me. What possible sexual gratification could a four-year-old child give a man? And how could I not know? What kind of mother am I? How could I be so blind not to pick up on any of this? Those questions stung me the most. There had to be an explanation. There just had to be!

The detectives had asked if I ever used the computer. I told them I hadn't. I'm not sure I even know how to turn it on. It was going to be Ralph's computer from the beginning. We bought it with the intention that he would use it primarily for business. I was with him when it bought it along with the printer, scanner, and other stuff. "Everything had to be top of the line," Ralph said. It was all top dollar as well. He kept telling me it was a business investment. That I could understand. But child pornography...?

The detectives asked me more than once if I knew what was on the computer. I shrugged. "Business accounts." I really had no idea. How many different ways could I tell them that? Why would they continue to ask me things I knew nothing about?

Robin was getting hungry. I wanted the detectives to leave. They had upset me enough. I also wondered why Ron Liebman hadn't returned my call. Surely, he checked in with his office. I had said it was urgent. Ralph was going to be furious with me.

"Look, I have nothing more to say to you and must give my daughter her dinner."

"All right, Mrs. Canby, we'll be on our way," Detective O'Brien said and both men rose from their chairs. "We'll most likely be in touch."

As I closed the door behind them, the telephone began to ring. I rushed to answer hoping it was our lawyer.

"Hello, Jane. What's going on?" Ron Liebman, our lawyer, asked.

"Nancy said you sounded frantic."

"I am. The police just left. Ralph was arrested earlier."

"On what charge?"

"Are you sitting?"

"What did he do, shoot another driver?"

"I wish that were it. It's child pornography—-"

"What?"

"I know. I can't believe it, either."

"Okay, tell me everything that happened and all you know."

I gave Ron a quick review of all that had taken place that afternoon. He interrupted every so often to ask a pertinent question.

"Okay, Jane, sit tight. I'm going down there to see if I can get him back by tonight. I'll keep you posted."

"Thanks, Ron."

"No, problem. Don't worry about a thing."

"I won't now that you're on your way."

Trying to push my anxiety to the back of my mind, I fed Robin. As she ate, I kept getting terrible flashes of pictures of Ralph abusing her. I was letting my anxiety use my imagination to create these terrible thoughts. All because in the back of my mind a little voice kept asking, "What if it is true?" Only, I refused to answer it.

Almost four hours later, Ron Liebman called back with news. Needless to say, I was beside myself at that time. I expected him to tell me that he was bringing Ralph home. He didn't. Instead, what he had to say made the little voice that was tormenting me seem more credible.

"There was a great deal of hard evidence removed from Ralph's computer, enough to arraign him. The judge found the charges appalling because a child was involved and granted the D.A. the enormous amount of bail that she requested."

"How much was the bail set for?"

"A million."

"Oh, God! We can't afford that."

"He'll have to remain in jail until his trial because of it."

"But he's no flight risk."

"That wasn't why the D.A. requested the amount."

"Huh?"

"She did it so Ralph wouldn't be anywhere near Robin."

"But I need Ralph to help me with Robin."

"That's out of the question. Is there some other family member who can help?"

"I don't know. I'll have to think of something. But, what about Ralph?"

"I've done all I can for him down here. I have to come up with some defense to try and get him off. Unfortunately for him, he's given new meaning to 'a picture says a thousand words.'"

"Can I see him?"

"I wouldn't advise it now. I'll let you know when."

"What can I do so I don't lose my mind?"

"Leave everything to me. We'll get through this."

"Thanks, Ron."

Because most of our assets were tied up in Ralph's business, I knew there was no way we'd be able to raise the necessary bail money. I could just imagine him fuming in jail. I felt awful for him. I still didn't believe that he was capable of doing such terrible things to any child let alone his own daughter. I kept my faith in him until the day they came to arrest me.

My sister took a leave of absence from her job to help me take care of Robin. I couldn't be any more grateful. It made things easier for me when I had to go for treatments. I often came back in worse condition than I was before I went.

A few days before Ralph's trial, the two detectives returned. Apologetically they told me that they had to take me down to the police station for further questioning.

"What for?" my sister asked. "She told you everything."

They had already met my sister on an earlier occasion and there was no love between them.

"We have our orders," Detective O'Brien replied coldly.

"And like the good little Nazis you are, you'll follow them."

"Karen, I don't think we should make things any more difficult than they are."

"Jane, did you ever have a backbone?"

"What good is it to argue? I'll go answer their questions and then I'll come home."

"Something's not right. Why do you have to go down there? Why don't you ask your measly questions here?"

"We would have gotten to that if you hadn't butted in," Detective O'Brien retorted.

"Hasn't she been through enough? She's not physically well, to begin with, and that sleaze of a husband of hers goes and sodomizes his own child—"

"Karen!"

My sister and Ralph had never gotten along. She'd never cared for him. That was the main reason I didn't see much of her after I got married.

The detectives explained that the D.A. wanted to speak to me. I hoped that somehow I might be able to help Ralph. Even so, as I got my coat and left with the detectives, I wasn't certain that there was anything new that I could tell them. Had I known what lay in store for me, I would have never gone into the car so willingly.

It turns out that my loving husband had told the D.A. that I knew about what he was doing and sometimes even held Robin down for him. He showed me pictures from the internet and I got turned on from viewing them. Of course, I denied all this. I couldn't understand how Ralph could lie. Perhaps he was offered a lighter sentence. The shock of this devastated me. First that he admitted his guilt and second that he implicated me.

Before the D.A. came to question me, I was attended to by the detectives. They didn't believe that I was involved. They had gone out of their way to help me and provided evidence to shed doubt on Ralph's story. They created a chart matching the times I went into the hospital with the dates on the downloaded pictures.

"How can I ever thank you for the trouble you've gone through to help me, especially after the things my sister had said?"

"Because we believe you're innocent and have gone through enough. We want to get scum like your husband off the street, but not at your expense," Detective O'Brien said.

"But what will I do if the D.A. believes Ralph?"

"I doubt if they will after they speak to you."

The D.A. and the A.D.A. questioned me for hours. I don't think they really believed Ralph.

"Do I need a lawyer?" I asked.

"Do you feel you need one?"

"I didn't do anything wrong. I would have killed Ralph if I had seen him touch my baby. It's obscene. But if I'm going to be railroaded and charged with aiding and abetting him, maybe I do."

The D.A. was a crusty-looking man who could be anyone's grandfather. The A.D.A. was about my age and a woman. She did most of the talking at first. They did everything to make me feel more comfortable. I guess they noticed how nervous I was.

"Either you're one of the greatest actresses alive or you are sick at heart at what you've learned about your husband," Carol Stein, the A.D.A., said to me. "I don't envy you."

"I would love to see him rot in jail. There's no way I could ever let him back in my life. The thought of him touching me again sickens me."

"We will try and convince a jury to convict him on all of the fifty counts. He'll be in jail for the next 280 years," Carol Stein said.

It was the evidence that the two detectives presented to the office of the District Attorney that convinced them of my innocence and I was never arrested or charged. A child psychologist examined Robin and confirmed she'd been abused. Robin admitted that her daddy touched her and taught her to touch him. She said that she was never allowed to tell me. What a secret my poor child was asked to keep.

I began to take Robin to a child psychologist for help. I only hoped she wasn't going to be scarred for life. I only prayed that I'd be around to see Robin grow up. Only time would tell. But then again, I was a fighter.

The End

BENEATH THE VELVET BLUE MOON

By Candace Gold

"Which star do you want to wish on, Nadine?" Father asked as we leaned against the railing, gazing up at the brilliant star-studded summer sky.

I pointed to the brightest and we each made a wish.

Sometimes when there were two full moons in one month—Blue Moons—which happened approximately every two and a half years, we made special wishes. All my wishes were special to me, for I always wished for a handsome prince to come and sweep me off my feet. However, I was willing to wait until I grew up.

***

In the summer of my nineteenth year, my wish came true. That was when I met Michael Greene. Michael was everything I'd dreamed my prince would be and we spent those sun-kissed days together. I have to admit, though, we met in a most unconventional way.

On the second day of our vacation, my parents, both English professors, were fast at work on the novel they were co-authoring. Basically, that left me pretty much on my own. I grabbed my beach bag and scribbled a note telling them I'd gone to the small beach on the other side of the lake. Chances were I'd be back before they even read the note, anyway. I only liked to bask, not bake, in the sun. Being a redhead with fair skin, my freckles didn't need new relatives.

I found a nice spot not too far from the water and spread out my blanket. Then I took my book from the bag, stretched out on my stomach, and began to read. Suddenly, out of nowhere, something hit the sand a few inches from my nose.

"What the...!"

"I'm so sorry," a deep male voice said as a hand reached out to help me to a sitting position.

I couldn't actually see him because I had sand in my eyes, not to mention the ton that found its way into the top of my bathing suit.

"Stay right there—don't move. I'll be right back," he said.

I tried to shake some of the sand off me in the few moments he was gone. He returned with wet towels and gently began to wipe the sand off my face. I opened my eyes to find myself gazing into beautiful eyes.

"Better, huh?" he asked.

"Much." I took the towel from him and wiped the sand from my shoulders and chest. Now that I could see again, I took in the rest of him, from the tussled full head of blue-black hair hanging over his forehead, the straight nose, and dimpled chin, to his muscled arms and chest. In my wildest dreams, I couldn't have conjured up a more handsome guy.

He grabbed the offending missile—a volleyball—and apologized again. "Look, it was an accident. I'm really okay."

Before he could reply, another guy with bronzed skin and windblown hair trotted over. "Hey, you coming back to play?"

My handsome stranger wrinkled his nose and shook his head. "Nah. Play without me," he replied, tossing the ball to the other guy.

"Catch you later," the guy said as he ran off with the ball.

"I'd like to make it up to you. Can I buy you a drink or something to eat at the snack bar?"

"My mother told me never to go off with strangers," I teased.

He smacked his forehead. "Forgive me for not introducing myself. I'm Michael Greene," he said, extending his hand.

I shook his hand and said, "I'm Nadine Stone."

He grinned, his green eyes twinkling. "Now that we're no longer strangers, how about getting something to eat at the snack bar?"

"I really should clean up first."

"No. I don't want to waste a moment."

"I'll only be a few minutes," I protested.

"You might disappear before I can learn everything there is to know about you."

"All right, you win," I said and walked with him to the snack bar.

He bought franks, French fries, and soda for us to eat under the umbrella at one of the small tables. I hadn't realized how hungry I was and quickly took a bite. I must have gotten some mustard on my nose because Michael smiled as he took a napkin and wiped it off. A strange vision passed in front of me of my own child asking Michael what he remembers most about me. I can hear the reply now. "Forever wiping off your mother's face. It always seems to get in the way of things."

"Tell me, who are you, Nadine Stone?" he asked, bringing me back to the present where I vowed to be neater.

"Nobody special. I'm starting my sophomore year in college this September."

"Have any idea what you want to do when you finish?" he asked before taking another healthy bite of his frank. He must have been just as hungry as I.

"I'm not sure. Maybe teaching, maybe research. What about you?"

"I'm finishing my senior year. Architecture's my thing. It was probably those Lincoln Logs my parents bought me when I was a kid."

I chuckled. "You must have designed luxury cabins."

"Not quite. I guess it's in my genes. My dad's an architect, too."

"Well, if genes count, then I'll end up a teacher. Both my parents are English professors. They're hard at work, as we speak, writing the great American novel this summer."

"Together?" he asked looking skeptical.

I nodded. "They're pretty close."

"I hope they remain that way after the summer is over," Michael said.

I smiled, understanding fully what he meant. I wanted to be alone with him, too.

"So, you'll be here the entire summer, Nadine?"

"Yes. How about you?"

"Two of my buddies from school rented a cabin for the summer with me. Sort of our last fling before plunging into the real world."

I wanted to know everything there was to know about Michael. As we sat talking, I suddenly became conscious of the rhythm of my heart. It seemed to be beating at a dangerously fast rate. I feared if it beat any faster it would crash right through me. If he could have this effect on me by only talking, I found myself wondering what would happen if he kissed me? Was there such a thing as love at first sight? I'd never given it much thought until that day, for I'd already fallen in love with Michael Greene.

Being with Michael every day made all ordinary things, like hiking and biking magical. Of course, my parents weren't totally unaware of what was going on, nor were they completely thrilled. My mother felt she needed to caution me. Knowing I was with Michael every day caused her parental radar to go off the screen. Instead of just coming out and saying what she actually meant, she used figures of speech and euphemisms. I found it somewhat amusing that she seemed so uncomfortable.

I was halfway out of the cabin one morning when she stopped me. "Nadine, I'd like to talk with you a moment."

I turned around and faced her.

"Are you on your way to meet Michael?"

"We're going bike riding around the trails. Why?"

"You'll be careful, of course."

"I'm *always* careful, Mom. And the bike is sturdy."

She had such a look of frustration on her face. "*We're* concerned about you."

"Don't—"

"Seeing someone everyday...well..."

"Stop worrying. I'm a *big* girl now."

"*That's* why we're worrying."

Obviously, my mother was speaking for my father as well, hence, the use of the pronoun *we*. I knew exactly what they were thinking and worded my reply carefully.

"You and Dad brought me upright. I can tell the difference between what's right and what's wrong. You've instilled in me the smarts needed to make rational choices. So why are you doubting yourselves, now?"

She pursed her lips in thought as she mulled over what I'd said. I'd taken the worrisome wind from her sails and she gave me a less harried, anemic smile. Then I blew her sails into a tailspin when I half-teased, "I love him, Mom. And I'm going to marry him. See ya later."

I left my poor mother standing there wondering whether or not she should chain me to my bed. I might have been kidding with her then, but in my heart, I meant every word. I'd meant what I said about being grown up. I knew what I felt for Michael had to be love. I'd never felt this way about any guy before. The very thought of him had the power to lift my spirits and make my heart soar. I may have spent nearly every summer of my life at Lake Flint, but with Michael, I felt as if I were seeing it for the first time. I suddenly became aware of the quiet beauty of the place. I discovered more to do and see than merely hanging out at the lake or beach.

One beautiful summer's night in early August, Michael and I walked along the lake holding hands. We stopped by the rail where my father and I had made our wishes when I was a child. A gentle breeze ruffled his hair as he smiled down at me. I smiled back at him. He drew me close and covered my mouth with his. Then he turned to look at the full moon.

"Look, Nadine, it's a Blue Moon."

"My father told me that anything you wished for under a Blue Moon always came true," I said.

"Always?" he asked with the mischievous little smile I found adorable.

"That's what he said."

"Then let's make wishes." His eyes were like emeralds, twinkling in the moonlight.

We closed our eyes and made wishes. I wished to be with Michael forever. Since you couldn't tell anyone your wish or it wouldn't come true, I didn't know what he'd wished for, but by the look on his face, I had a pretty good idea.

"Promise, Nadine...promise me on that Blue Moon that you'll meet me here next year."

"I promise," I said.

Then, under that magnificent moon, we sealed our pledge to meet with a kiss. If I could have put that moment into a bottle and saved it forever, I would have. I had been granted my childhood wish. My handsome prince stood there before me. And no matter what, I knew with all my heart I would always love Michael.

We swapped telephone numbers. I'd keyed his into my cell phone. We'd stay in touch while we both went back to school. And perhaps, if time permitted, get together during the holidays.

That night of promise turned out to be the last night we'd spend together. The next morning, my grandmother called my mother with terrible news. My grandfather had been rushed to the hospital. He'd had a heart attack. I'd hastily said goodbye to Michael. The tears in my eyes were for Michael, but my concern was for my grandfather.

We drove directly to the airport and booked a flight to Arizona. From the airport, we went straight to the hospital. My grandfather was already in the operating room when we got there. We found my grandmother sitting in the waiting room, her eyes red and swollen from crying. My mother tried to comfort her but ended up adding her own tears to the mix. It took another two hours before the doctor came to speak with us.

"Mrs. Carlson, if he gets through the night, he's going to be all right."

A collective sigh of relief could be heard after he gave us this prognosis. He then proceeded to explain what he'd done in the operating room. My grandfather was a feisty old man. Even though Grandpa wasn't out of the woods just yet, we were given hope. I knew that if anyone was going to pull through a quadruple bypass it would be him. We were allowed to peek in on him before we all went to my grandparent's place to spend the night.

The following morning, we returned to the hospital to see him. He was fully awake and though his voice was dry and gravelly, he managed to bark orders to the nurses. Though his skin still bore a gray cast, we knew he was on the mend. And that's what counted.

My parents and I remained in Arizona with my grandmother until my grandfather was able to go home. It wasn't long before he was his usual cantankerous self. He was very political and extremely opinionated. He was forever writing scorching letters to the local newspapers. I guess, no one ever told him it could be dangerous to discuss politics. To tell the truth, when my grandmother had told my mother that Grandpa was in the hospital, I actually thought that somebody had shot him.

We returned to New York in time for the beginning of the new semester. That's about the time I realized I couldn't find my cell phone. For me, it was a category five disaster. It contained every important telephone number—including Michael's.

My father found me in my room ransacking all my bags, dumping everything out, as I frantically searched for my phone.

"What's going on, Nadine? This place looks like it was hit by a bomb," he said.

I must've had a panic-stricken expression on my face when I looked up because his demeanor changed quickly to one of concern.

"What's wrong, honey?"

The pent-up tears began to stream down my cheeks. "I think I lost my cell phone."

"Don't worry. I'll call the carrier and discontinue your service. We'll get you another phone."

"You don't understand..." I whined as more tears welled in my eyes.

"Honey, we'll replace it. Losing your cell phone should be the worst thing that ever happens to you."

"It is."

"You're right, I don't understand," he said running his fingers through his hair.

"It was my phone book. Michael's number was in it. And now it's gone..."

As if a curtain of uncertainty had just lifted from his eyes, my father took me in his arms and held me as I sobbed on his shoulder. I could tell we were both on the same page now.

"Sweetheart, he'll find a way to get in touch with you."

My father contacted the carrier and let them know I'd lost my phone. I purchased another a few days later. I thought about what my father said. If Michael was going to find a way to contact me, he'd have to be very creative. I now had a new cell phone number and hadn't given him my home number, which is unlisted. My parents didn't want a ton of calls from students.

I tried to get in touch with Michael but hit a dead end. I was beside myself. How do you meet the man of your dreams only to lose him? The last resort would have to be the summer. Would Michael still keep his promise and come? I never got the chance to find out.

A few weeks before Christmas, my parents were killed instantly in an auto accident caused by a drunk who'd run a red light. We'd started the day, as usual, having breakfast together. Had I known it would be the last time I'd ever see them alive; I would've said all the things I should've told them and held them close. However, I'm no seer and can hardly deal with the present than be able to read the future. I've been told nothing is instant, not even pudding. Well, they were wrong. I was an instant orphan. An only child, I didn't even have siblings with whom to share my grief. All I had were my grandparents who flew out to be with me.

It's difficult for me to retell what actually happened from the moment the police came to my door with the news about my mother and father to the days following their funeral because I was in some kind of suspended animation. I knew I wasn't taking their deaths well. In truth, I didn't care. I didn't want to feel. I wanted to believe it was all some stupid nightmare I'd awake from and they'd be still alive.

My grandparents put my house on the market and whisked me back to Arizona with them. During this time I was a caterpillar living in a cocoon of my own making. My grandparents tried everything they could to bring me out of it, but I resisted. It was easier to sulk and feel sorry for myself. Then I met one of their neighbors, Charlotte White.

Charlotte was somewhat younger than my grandparents. I guessed her age to be around fifty-seven. She had a pleasant, round face, permanently lined from always smiling. The gray streaks in her hair were becoming and she wore her age well. However, it was the inner beauty that made her special. Whether or not our meeting at the pool was planned by my grandmother or pure chance, I'll never know. I'm truly glad we had the opportunity to talk.

When my parents' lives were snuffed out like a candle, I had trouble dealing with it because of the way I'd always viewed things. I've never considered myself a deep thinker. Solving the world's problems, I left to my grandfather and others. But I always believed things happened for the best. It's my version of looking at the glass being half-full as opposed to half-empty. I'd tried to find the silver lining or good in everything.

I had a great deal of help in doing so from my father who was a born optimist if ever there was one.

However, I couldn't find any good in the death of my parents. My entire world had come undone. There was no longer any rhyme or reason to my life. And like my world, I simply came apart at the seams. Until my meeting with Charlotte.

She had lived in Los Angeles, a single mother trying to bring up three kids. Her husband, a construction worker, had died in a freak accident leaving no insurance money. This forced Charlotte to work two jobs in order to keep a roof over her family's head and food on the table. She found it difficult but had no choice. Her oldest son joined a gang and was killed. The middle child got hooked on drugs, while her youngest was killed in a drive-by shooting. Her world imploded. As she put it, "I didn't just hit bottom, I lived there. I crawled into a bottle of vodka and grew gills."

Looking at her the day we met, I couldn't believe she was the same person she'd just described. She'd had more than her share of tragedy and loss in her life to last three lifetimes and yet she'd pulled herself together and moved on with her life. What was my excuse?

"Don't look so amazed. I found my answer in the Lord. With Jesus' help, I found the strength to stop drinking and help my Jared kick his habit."

No, I didn't find my answer or salvation in religion. Instead, following my conversation with Charlotte, I took a hard look at myself in the mirror. I didn't like what I saw. I'm certain my parents weren't happy with me, either. They were probably furious with me for feeling so sorry for myself. Knowing my dad, he'd want me to get on with my life.

I enrolled in the local college and soon decided to become a paralegal. I'd begun a new chapter in my life; one I knew would please my parents. And no, I never forgot Michael. He would always remain in a special part of my heart.

***

I landed a job at a prominent law firm in Phoenix. There were five partners, fifteen lawyers and three paralegals, including me. At twenty-two, I was the youngest of the paralegals. The other two women were in their late thirties. They took me under their wings telling me which lawyers to be wary of and which to definitely avoid.

There was one lawyer, in particular, who seemed to be off their radar—Josh Thompson. I met him at my first office Christmas party, which I hadn't wanted to attend at first. Since Michael, I hadn't really dated much and found I didn't care one way or the other. Molly, one of the other paralegals practically twisted my arm.

"Coming to the office Christmas party, Nadine?" she asked during lunch one day.

"No."

"Why not?"

"Don't want to," I replied quickly.

She came back at me immediately. "You never go out. What kind of life is that?"

"Mine. And I like it just fine, thank you very much."

She rolled her eyes at me. "Well, it's about time you started dating again. A pretty girl like you...damn! A nun gets more action."

My face grew hot at her implication, but I managed to say, "I like the way things are."

"How could you? It's as if you're watching the world go by from the other side of the window."

Despite Molly's butting into my personal life, I truly liked her. She'd been a good friend to me from the first day I'd started with Thompson, Brown, St. Charles, Gould and Woodward. She was always there when I needed help and advice. She also knew about Michael. I'd hoped she'd respect my feelings on the matter of dating and my desire not to get involved with another man.

"Just come to keep me company," she said.

With all she'd done for me, it seemed the least I could do, so I gave in and said, "All right."

"Great." She hugged me, nearly sucking all the air from my lungs. All I wanted was for her to release me so I could breathe again.

***

When Molly and I walked into the employee lounge where the party was being held, the room was already filled with people, buzzing with the cacophony of a dozen different conversations. My gut instinct was to turn around and run. Unfortunately, Molly sensed this and took hold of my arm. "Let's go to the bar and get something to drink. After all, this *is* a party."

We got our drinks and moved off to the side. The room became more crowded and we somehow got separated. This was the last thing I'd wanted to happen. I backed my way into a corner where I'd feel safer. I didn't mind being alone. However, I soon discovered I wasn't.

A male voice behind me said, "I see you love crowds nearly as much as I do."

I turned to face a tall, pleasant-looking man in a navy-blue pinstriped suit. For a split second, he reminded me of Michael, with his dark good looks. The smiling eyes I looked into were blue, not green.

"Is this your first office Christmas party?" he asked.

I nodded.

"Thought so. I'm Josh Thompson, not to be confused with the partner. Couldn't even get him to adopt me."

I laughed, already liking this man.

"I'm Nadine Stone and probably even lower than you on the food chain."

"Why you have the distinguished look of a lawyer," he replied.

Smiling, I told him I was only a paralegal.

"Don't sell yourself short. Without your work, the cogs of this fine institution wouldn't get oiled."

"Thanks for being nice."

"My fair lady, nice doesn't come into the picture. I was merely being honest. Come, let's refresh our drinks and go sit somewhere and talk. We have a great deal of catching up to do."

Josh and I talked the afternoon away and had dinner together. He was a nice guy and I enjoyed his company. We shared many things in common, especially heartbreak. He was coming out of a relationship that had gone sour after a year-and-a-half. He'd thought she was everything he wanted until he discovered she led a secret life. A sales rep for a large pharmaceutical company, she traveled a great deal. Josh had no idea she had lovers in different states. He discovered this by accident.

"She'd mentioned she had a convention in Las Vegas. Since it was her birthday and I'd never been to Vegas, I decided to go surprise her. Only, I was the one who was surprised."

"What happened?" I asked, leaning closer.

"Well, I was told by the front desk clerk she wasn't in her room. I figured she might've gone out to dinner and decided to have a drink while I waited for her to return. I walked into one of the bars and nearly freaked."

"She was there?"

"Oh, she was there all right. She was in the corner giving some man a lap dance."

"Did you confront her?"

"Not just then. I had a couple of drinks while I tried to calm down. I didn't want to commit murder in front of all those witnesses. I waited until they left and followed them up to her room. Now I was certain."

"So you banged on her door and..."

"Nope. I had a better idea."

This was like a suspense novel. I was hooked and couldn't wait to hear what Josh had done.

"I went home and waited for her to return. She had no idea I knew about Vegas. I'd used my cell phone to take pictures of her with this guy and blew up the pictures. I hung them up over my bed. You should have seen her face when she saw them."

"Just like one of those MasterCard commercials, priceless?"

"Exactly. She couldn't deny it. Spitefully, she told me about the other men. How I didn't strangle her, right then and there, is a miracle."

I knew that woman had hurt Josh badly, for even now as he retold the story, I could detect pain in his eyes. I found myself telling him about Michael. In a way we were kindred spirits and became close friends, often having dinner or getting together on the weekends.

In the blink of an eye, two years had flown by. Josh and I grew closer. My grandparents loved him and envisioned us getting married. I loved Josh, but it wasn't the same kind of love I'd had for Michael. It could only be characterized as a comfortable relationship, with no bells ringing or whistles going off. If I married him, I knew I'd never want for anything. He'd be a good husband, faithful and loving. However, as good as it sounded, I felt something was missing.

Josh and I talked about the possibility of marriage, only it was always just that, talk. We didn't go beyond. Perhaps he sensed my hesitancy or was uncertain himself. However, as time wore on, I knew we were heading down that path.

As August approached, Josh found himself wondering where his life was heading and shared these thoughts with me.

"It's time I settled down and began to raise a family. Want to help?"

"Are you asking me to marry you?"

"Yeah, if you'll have me."

I didn't answer right away.

"Are you still unsure?"

"Maybe."

"Not a problem."

I was confused. "What are you getting at?"

"I'm going to be tied up with a pretty big case. Why don't you take a vacation and go cool off somewhere and think about us," he suggested.

I realized it wasn't fair for me to go on indefinitely as we were. Either I wanted to marry him or not. Absence made the heart grow fonder, didn't it? I kissed him goodbye and took a flight back to Lake Flint. I hadn't been there in years. The change of scenery would do me good.

I closed the book I'd tried to read and stared out the window. My mind drifted back to that last magical summer I'd spent with Michael. I'd accepted the fact a long time ago that I'd never see him again. And yet, I knew I'd never truly gotten over him any more than I'd forgotten him. So many times during the passing years I thought of him and often wondered where he was and if he'd thought of me. Perhaps going back now I'd be able to close that chapter of my life and be able to marry Josh.

At the airport, I rented a car and drove to the lake. I was lucky to get a cabin for the week. As I drove toward the resort, I noticed changes along the highway. There were more restaurants and strip malls, leaving hardly any open land. The signs of progress, I mused. I rounded the lake. It looked smaller than I'd remembered. The cabins looked older and could've used a fresh coat of paint. Children were playing on the swings at the small playground and several seasonal fishermen were fishing from small boats. In my mind's eye, I saw myself riding bikes with Michael around the lake.

Stop it! I scolded myself. I came to think about Josh, not Michael. I went to my cabin and unpacked my things. I could almost hear my parents moving about in the other room. Tears welled in my eyes. I still missed them. I blinked away the tears and left the cabin to get something to eat. The manager of the restaurant had gotten older. He still reminded me of Vincent Price, but not in a creepy way. I was surprised when he remembered me.

I had a grilled cheese sandwich and coffee and read a local newspaper. Families came in for a bite and I wondered if the kids knew how lucky they were to have a family. One thing I'd learned the last several years was life is so very precious. It's the one commodity you can't replace. I finished my sandwich and returned to the cabin. It had been an early flight and I was exhausted.

After dinner, I strolled to the lake and leaned against the railing—the wishing railing. It was a beautiful night. The sky was blanketed with twinkling stars, reminding me of the times my father and I would wish on a star together. I realized as the full moon rose in the sky that it was a blue one. Dad had insisted all wishes made on a Blue Moon were special and always came true. Even though I no longer believed it, I decided to make a wish anyway. I'd intended to wish that Josh and I would have a long and happy marriage, but instead of saying Josh, I said Michael. I laughed at my own Freudian slip.

Suddenly from behind me, a voice said, "I'd never forgotten that laugh."

My heart began to beat in triple time as I turned to face the man whose infectious smile I'd never forgotten, either.

"Michael?"

"You're more beautiful than I remembered," he said moving closer.

"Am I really seeing you, or have I conjured you up?" I asked.

He chuckled. "I'm really here, Nadine. I knew if I waited long enough, you'd return, too."

Tears welled in my eyes as I touched his face. He took my hand and brought it to his lips.

"I couldn't reach you during that year and thought I'd see you in the summer..." he began.

As the tears slipped from my eyes, he kissed each and every one of them.

"My parents were killed, and I lost your phone number. I'm so sorry."

"You're here now. Nothing else matters," he said as he kissed my trembling lips.

When we broke apart, all I could manage to say was, "Oh, Michael, Michael..." before his lips recaptured mine, once more. "I never thought I'd ever see you again," I whispered. "I can't believe you're actually here with me now."

"I love you, Nadine. I always have and I always will. This time, I'm not letting you get away."

Michael scooped me up into his arms and carried me into his cabin. We made sweet love and like magic, the years and distance melted away as we were transported back to the golden summer we first met.

I now knew what was missing from the relationship I'd had with Josh. It was the fire and passion I found with Michael. I also knew I would return to Phoenix with a different answer from the one he expected. I didn't want to hurt him, but my life belonged in New York with Michael. It had been ordained. After all, wishes made under the magic of a Blue Moon always came true.

The End

A MURDERER GAVE ME THE GIFT OF LIFE

by Candace Gold

My father left my mother when I was eight and my brother, Darrell, was six. To keep a roof over our heads and food on the table, my grandmother moved in with us while Mom worked two jobs. It turned out that Grandma needed more of a keeper than we did.

She liked her whiskey. "Takes the bumps out of the day's road," she'd often say. Half the time when we'd come home from school, we'd find her sacked out in her favorite chair snoring. If we were able to wake her, she'd cook dinner. If not, it was up to me to see that we ate. By the time Mama came home, both Darrell and I were asleep. We'd get to see her only on Sundays when she was off from both jobs.

Darrell grew up angry at everyone. He ran with the wrong crowd and got arrested at fourteen for breaking into a home and stealing a stereo and TV. Too bad the owner had insured both items and their serial numbers were on file. My brother got busted when he had written his

real name and address on the pawnshop receipt.

He was sent to a place for troubled teens. Instead of getting straightened out, Darrell only got worse. When he came out, I hardly recognized the person he'd become. From that day on, Darrell came and went as he pleased. I lived with the constant fear that he'd get himself in trouble again, or worse, killed one day. He refused to listen to my advice. My mother had already given up on him. "No good bum," she'd say to him. "Just like your father."

That comparison would make him furious and he'd storm out of the apartment. One day he got so mad that he nearly hit her. I'm sorry to admit I was actually glad when he stayed away.

I'd gotten a job as a receptionist in a large insurance agency and managed to save a few bucks a week. I intended to move out when I could afford it.

***

One evening when I walked into the apartment, I found the TV on as usual. Grandma was sitting in her favorite chair, only she wasn't snoring. The whiskey bottle on the coffee table was still full. Walking over to her I saw that she was staring into nothingness. I gently shook her but got no response. A thin line of drool clung to the corner of her mouth. "Grandma! Wake up!" Panic slowly spidered down my spine as I ran to the phone and called 911. I had just hung up when I heard the creaking of Darrell's bedsprings. I rushed into his room to tell him about Grandma.

I stopped short. My jaw dropped when I saw what he was doing. He looked up, noticing me just then, as well.

"Get the hell out!"

He did not lessen the tension on his belt that he had wrapped around his arm. Nor did he lower the syringe poised to jab his jutting vein.

"No, Darrell! Please don't!" I pleaded with him.

"Mind your own business," he growled.

"I can't. You're my brother."

"I ain't your responsibility."

The look on his face said it all. When he set his jaw and glared, I knew it was no use. Darrell could be as stubborn as a mule. And just as stupid. No use fighting with him. It was like spitting in the wind.

Two cops patrolling the neighborhood took the call. I let them in.

"It's my grandmother," I said pointing.

The taller cop went over to check her. "Alive. Possible stroke or cardiac arrest."

"Anyone else here?" the shorter cop asked, already half-way out of the room.

"Just my brother," I said to his vanishing back.

A moment later, all hell broke loose, changing everything. The cops busted my brother for the possession of an illegal substance. Darrell blamed me for the cops showing up, thinking I'd called them on him. He hadn't known that Grandma had suffered a stroke. He just refused to ever speak to me again.

Mama came home and found me crying in the living room. I was surprised she was home so early.

"What you blubbering about, girl?"

"Grandma. She okay?"

"How should I know if she's here with you?"

"Didn't they tell you?"

"Who? Where's the old bat, anyway?" she asked noticing the empty chair.

"I gave the cops your work number..."

"Where is she? What she do, drink herself to death?"

"That's not funny. They took her to the hospital. Said they'd call you."

I found myself suddenly angry at the policemen. Perhaps they were too busy arresting Darrell and forgot.

"That number ain't no good. I don't work there no more."

"Why didn't you tell me you changed jobs?"

"Slipped my mind. Doesn't matter none since it's hard to reach me at this new job."

"Where do you work now, mama?"

"That's none of your concern."

Seeing how she was dressed; I knew what kind of job my mother had. Some job, a nice way to find out, too. What a messed-up family I belonged to. All the more reason to get the hell out. If I didn't, I'd be destroyed along with the rest of them.

Grandma died during the night. Mama went to the hospital to say goodbye. I didn't want to. There'd be enough time at her funeral.

***

Darrell got a harsh sentence because of his past priors. Afterward, he turned around in the courtroom and locked eyes with me. I felt the heat of his smoldering stare.

"Rot in hell, Darlene!" he shouted as he was led away.

Those terrible words hurt. I meant him no harm. I'd loved my brother and cared for him more than his own mother did, who hadn't even shown up. She was probably too busy selling her body.

When I tried to visit him later on in prison, he wouldn't see me. I'd finally lost my brother. The day after my brother was sentenced, I moved out of the apartment. When mama eventually showed up, she'd find out I was gone for good. I didn't bother leaving a note. I didn't want her to know where I was—not that she'd come after me.

This hadn't been a spur of the moment move. I'd been planning to get out for a long time, putting away every spare nickel I had. Even though my job was decent, I still needed more if I were going to support myself. I had to become an agent.

My chance to move up the food chain at the insurance agency came when one of the agents was killed in a tragic accident and his position needed to be filled. Realizing that this was my moment and I might not get another chance, I went to speak to the owner, Charles Reilly.

Charles Reilly was in his late fifties. What little hair that remained on his head was hardly discernable from his scalp. His heavy eyelids gave him a dull-witted look, but he was hardly that, having started the business from his home and eventually expanding it into one of the biggest insurance companies in town.

"Mr. Reilly, may I please speak to you?" I asked trying steady my voice.

"Of course, Darlene."

"I'd like to fill John's position," I said getting right to the point.

"You would, would you?"

"I've learned a great deal about insurance, and I think I can do a good job."

"Well, I do prefer to promote from within. It doesn't hurt to give you a chance."

"Oh, thank you from the bottom of my heart," I gushed.

He smiled. "And if you're as good as you say we'll help you get licensed."

I let out a sigh of relief, feeling a hundred percent better than I did a few minutes ago.

"As soon as I fill your present position, you can get started."

"You won't regret this," I promised.

"Just remember, you can't afford to fail. You won't have a position to go back to."

***

A week later, I was learning the ropes from one of the other agents. Emily Dobbs, a middle-aged woman who always dressed well and made a great deal of money on commissions, so I paid close attention to everything she told me. As Mr. Reilly had said, I had to succeed. Losing my job and having to go back to my mother's apartment wasn't an option.

I worked hard and became a good agent. Passing the test to become licensed, I got a raise and a reason to become the best agent that I could. I began to bring in my own accounts and made good money from the commissions I received. Before long, I was able to afford the things I used to wish I had. I was also able to go out with the girls for a drink after work on Fridays. In fact, on one such night, I met Frank Benson.

Frank Benson was a tall, good-looking guy with thick black hair sitting at the bar with two other guys, watching a baseball game on one of the flat-screened plasma TVs. It was my turn to buy a round of beer for the three of us, Emily Dobbs, Carol Lang, a woman around my age, and myself. The bartender placed the mugs down in front of me. There was no way I could carry them all in one trip. Noticing my plight, Frank offered to carry one over to the table. I hadn't thought he even noticed me.

It wasn't long before he and I were deep in conversation. The other two girls had encouraged it. Emily, being a happily married woman, and Carol, engaged to be married soon, were always trying to fix me up with single men. They were thrilled that he had singled me out.

Frank Benson asked me out for the following evening. That became a turning point in my life and the first of many dates. He was an electrician and owned his own business. Divorced for five years, he was ready to move on.

"Until I saw you, Darlene, I hadn't given any thought to dating."

"I never really had time to date. I was too busy building a career for myself," I said.

"Then I lucked out."

"I think we both did, Frank."

***

It wasn't long before I fell in love with Frank Benson. He was wonderful, caring and decent. Nothing at all like the men in my family, speaking of which, I never told him about my family background for fear of ruining my chances with him. Six months from the day we met, Frank gave me an engagement ring. Wanting to start the year perfectly, we set a wedding date for the following New Year's Day.

For the next six years, life for us was filled with love and happiness. The only thing that we both desired and couldn't seem to have was a child. After trying for some time with little success, we began to discuss our options, checking out fertility doctors or adoption.

The first thing we did was put our name on several adoption lists. When I asked Frank why he wasn't so keen on going to a fertility doctor he replied, "I don't want to know whose fault it is. I don't want that to ever come between us."

I gave what he said some thought. I understood where he was coming from and never brought the subject up again. I loved him that much. He was my entire life. As long as I had him, I was happy.

***

My brother's trial was quite a media event. Because he'd killed the cashier of the convenience store he was robbing to pay for a fix, a pregnant woman and the mother of two small children, it made quite a human interest story. The bottom line was that it sold newspapers. However, it also caught Frank's attention.

"Say, this guy who killed those people, is he a relation?" he asked jokingly, expecting a no from me.

It was about time I told him the entire truth. I hadn't lied about my family. I just hadn't told Frank anything about them. I was too ashamed.

In a small voice, I said, "He's my brother."

Silence. A curtain of quiet dropped between us.

I had to tell him everything now. Over a pot of coffee, I told Frank about the family I grew up in. When I was finished, I felt as if a boulder had been lifted from my shoulders. Still, I feared that he wouldn't love me anymore. It might seem to be an irrational thought, but it was the foremost one kicking around in my mind at that moment.

Frank reached across the kitchen table and took my hand in his. "It's amazing."

"What?"

"That you turned out the way you did."

"I couldn't be like them. Life is much too precious to squander."

He nodded, pulling me into his arms. "I love you, Darlene," he whispered and kissed me. Together we walked into our bedroom and shut the rest of the world out.

My brother was found guilty and sentenced to death. My family tree was being stripped of its limbs. What did it matter? I hadn't spoken to my brother in ages. He'd transformed into a hardened criminal. What was there to say to one another now?

***

My beautiful, ordered world began to crack silently. Feeling tired and achy, I figured I was putting in too many hours at work. I decided to work fewer hours and spend more time at home. I soon found that I liked having more time to do the little things I always wanted to do like making special meals for the man I loved. Only my health didn't improve. I began to worry that something else might be wrong.

I finally made an appointment for a complete physical. Since my complaints were general in nature and could be from a number of causes, I was sent to a lab for a battery of blood and urine tests. My results came back a few days later. Only I wasn't home when the doctor's office called.

Frank and I were celebrating our ninth wedding anniversary at Willow Way Bed and Breakfast tucked away high on a ridge far from the hustle and bustle of town. We were having a wonderful time. It was like a honeymoon, being alone, just the two of us. I must admit that we spent most of the time in bed, which was just fine. If I got tired, I merely closed my eyes and went to sleep with Frank's strong loving arms around me.

I opened my eyes to find him staring into mine.

"Wiped you out, huh?" he said grinning.

"Yeah. You're my very own sex machine."

"Are you being sarcastic?"

"Nope! And I don't share. So, all you jealous women stay away."

He laughed and kissed my nose. I wanted to freeze this moment and keep it locked away in my memory forever.

Reluctantly, we returned home the following day. Our answering machine was filled with messages. Frank elected himself to listen to them all.

"Hey, Darlene!" Frank called to me.

"What?"

"There's a message from Dr. Green's office. They got your results back."

***

I called Dr. Green's office after I got to work. I wanted to hear my results by myself since I had this awful dread that something was terribly wrong with me. I didn't want to upset Frank, even though a little voice in the back of my head kept telling me that he'd know anyway.

"Dr. Green wants you to see him as soon as possible to discuss the results," the nurse informed me.

"Well, what is it?"

"The doctor will explain."

"Can't you tell me anything?" I heard the panic rising in my voice.

"All he said was to tell you to make an appointment," Mrs. Benson. "You'll have to speak with him."

"Fine. Transfer me to reception so I can make one."

By the time I'd hung up, I was miserable. I now envisioned the worst. Rerunning the entire conversation with the nurse in my mind, I hadn't noticed Emily standing by my desk.

"Are you all right?"

I nodded.

"Just checking. You had the most agonized look on your face."

"Nothing's wrong," I lied. Somehow, I don't think she actually believed me.

I found it hard to keep focused on my work. Luckily my appointment was for tomorrow. The hardest part was not acting worried in front of Frank.

***

Rather than cook I brought home take out. Stopping off at the Chicken Hut, I picked up enough food to feed four people. I wasn't hungry but thought that Frank might be. Sometimes he worked straight through the day without eating.

All he did was walk through the door that night, kiss me hello, and ask, "What happened with the doctor?" and I broke down and began to sob.

"Darlene, what is it?"

"I can't do this."

"Do what?"

"Go through this alone—I wanted to so I wouldn't get you upset, but look at me..."

"You shouldn't have to go through anything alone. We're a team, remember?"

"I'm so afraid."

"Shhh," he said putting his arms around me and rocking me as if I were a child. "What did the doctor say?"

"I didn't even see him yet. And I'm already falling apart."

"You're frightened and that's understandable. However, tomorrow you'll know more. It's the not knowing that's often the worst."

I realized that he was right. It didn't make me feel better, though.

"I'll go with you tomorrow. What time is your appointment?"

"12:30."

"No problem. I'll meet you there."

That night I lie awake thinking how lucky I was to have Frank. He wasn't perfect, constantly starting projects around the house and leaving them often unfinished. Neatness just wasn't a passion of his.

Luckily, I was. More importantly, he was faithful and came home to me every night. What would happen to him if I were to die?

***

I was still sitting in the waiting room, checking my watch every other minute when Frank walked in.

"Good, I'm not late," he said. He was breathless as if he'd run all the way to the office building from his truck.

He sat down next to me and took one of my hands in his and squeezed it. Five minutes later the nurse called my name. We rose together and followed her into the doctor's office. Dr. Green was reviewing my file.

"Mr. Benson, Darlene?"

Frank nodded and said, "Please call me Frank."

"I'm Philip Green," he said extending his hand.

Frank shook it. "How is my wife?"

"That's what we're here to discuss."

The next half hour had to be one of the worst thirty minutes of my life. The doctor explained the results of my tests. What it boiled down to was this: there were extremely high amounts of protein accumulated in various tissues throughout my body. Proteins are important in building muscles, bones, nails, and hair. They constantly circulate throughout the body in the blood. Normally they're harmless. However, sometimes cells produce abnormal proteins that can settle in body tissue, forming deposits and causing disease. These deposits are called amyloids and the disease process Amyloidosis. It could be genetic or be the result of another pathological condition."

Just like me to get a disease I'd never heard of. As I listened to Dr. Green it felt as if the moments of my life were ticking away, like sand in an hourglass.

"What's the treatment and prognosis?" Frank asked in a strange voice.

"Honestly, no effective treatment has been found to reverse the effects of Amyloidosis."

Great, I'm dead, I gasped, causing Frank to give my hand a gentle squeeze. However, no reassurance would help, for from that point on all I fixated on was the fact I was going to die.

"But we have drugs that may improve organ function and survival rates by interrupting the growth of these abnormal cells that produce amyloid protein."

"Like cancer medicine?" Frank asked.

The doctor nodded. "They're basically the same drugs used in chemotherapy to treat certain cancers."

"So, I'm going to go bald and vomit."

"Those are the possible side effects, yes."

"Is there anything else we have to know about this disease?" Frank asked.

"There were high levels of protein in Darlene's urine. Medically that's called proteinuria. Healthy kidneys prevent protein from entering the urine."

"So, there's something wrong with my kidneys, as well," I deduced.

"Yes. They're not working properly. This is all related, the doctor said."

By the time I left the doctor's office, I had an appointment for my first treatment. I wasn't looking forward to any of this. The thought of crawling into a corner and dying seemed mighty tempting and a great deal cheaper. However, then I'd imagined how my death would affect Frank and knew that I couldn't do that. For his sake, I had to try and fight this thing.

***

My life from this point on could be categorized according to stages. Of course, the first one started when I began treatment. To say that it was awful was an understatement. For two days afterward, I'd feel as if a herd of wild buffalos had stampeded over me. I began to dread going for my treatment. My hair had begun to fall out and I lost my eyebrows making me look like a freak. It all did wonders for my ego.

Frank began to make love to me less. I truly thought that he didn't love me anymore. I was afraid that one day I'd wake up and find him gone. I'd look in the mirror and I'd cry at the ghost of the person that looked back at me. Ironically, I felt worse than I had before I started. As a result, I became terribly depressed and didn't even want to leave the house. I guess this was when stage two began. I'd already taken a leave of absence from my job, so I had all the time in the world now. Or did I? Sometimes I hardly got out of bed. If I did, I never dressed. Instead, I lived in my nightclothes, which consisted of a T-shirt and loungers.

At this point, Frank feared to leave me alone and went to speak to the doctor. I discovered this when the chairwoman of a support group for people with debilitating diseases came to see me.

I opened the door to find a tall thin woman standing there. Immediately I was sorry that I had. "If you're going to try to sell me something, forget it."

"Darlene?"

"Yes."

"I'm Karen Winslow. Frank and Dr. Green asked me to stop by."

I began to get suspicious and annoyed. What were Frank and the doctor up to? Why couldn't they just let me be?

"For what?"

"To see how you're doing."

"Well, as you can see, I'm doing just dandy."

"You don't look that way," she replied ignoring my sarcasm.

"What would you know? You don't know me from Adam. Or should I say, Eve?"

"True, but I can tell a person in pain—anytime."

"Who *are* you? And why have you come?"

"May I come in?"

"I'm going to regret this, aren't I?"

"I certainly hope not."

"Look *who* I'm asking," I murmured to myself.

I led her to the kitchen and remembering my manners, asked if she'd like some coffee.

"Only if it's already made. I don't want you to fuss on my account."

I poured the coffee and took out some creamer from the refrigerator and put it on the table next to the sugar. Then I asked once more, "Why are you here?"

"Honestly, Frank is afraid that you're going to do harm to yourself."

"What would he care? He hasn't touched me in months." I couldn't believe that I actually blurted that out to a complete stranger.

"He probably was afraid to, not wanting to hurt you. If he didn't love you, I wouldn't be talking to you now. I'd like you to join our support group. We all have some kind of disease and lean on each other for strength to get through the tough times."

"I don't feel like joining a pity party, thank you very much."

"You'd rather stay here alone and feel sorry for yourself? Haven't you ever heard the saying, 'misery loves company?'"

Was she kidding or what? I wondered to myself.

"We try to help each other through a crisis. That's not pity, Darlene."

I couldn't control the tears that streamed down my face. Karen put her hands on my shoulders. "That's the girl, let it out. We all need a good cry every now and then. When you're done, hop into the shower and get dressed. There's a nice bunch of people I'd like you to meet."

That's when stage three clicked in. I allowed Karen to take me to the hospital where the support group met. There were fifteen men and women seated in a room. Some even looked worse than I did. The one common factor that united everyone was the fact that they were sick.

Each person introduced themselves to me and told me about their illness. I spoke about mine. Before long, I felt that I was among friends.

Okay, I didn't dance out of that room a happy lotto winner, but my spirits had lifted. As time passed, a few of these people would die and new ones would join. One woman told me that she never bought green bananas for fear that she wouldn't be around by the time they ripened. At first, I wondered how she could joke about death like that. In time, I understood.

*****

By the end of the second year, or phase four, my body seemed to be reacting favorably to a new drug that had just gotten FDA approval. Unfortunately, the amyloid deposits had already damaged one of my kidneys to the point that it no longer functioned. My other one worked, but poorly at best. I had been forced to undergo dialysis. Eventually, in order to go on living, I would need a kidney transplant.

It was at this point in my life, I figured time was running out for me. The problems with my kidneys were irreversible and worsening. I began to count every new day as a blessing. The list for kidney donations was quite a lengthy one. I figured that by the time it was my turn and they found a match for me, I'd no longer need it because I'd be dead.

*****

I had just gotten home from a dialysis session when my phone rang. It was a lawyer who was representing Darrell on one of his appeals. He'd been on death row for about seven years now.

I was shocked when this lawyer, who called himself Robert Burnside, told me that Darrell wanted to see me. We hadn't spoken since his first conviction, years ago.

"Why does my brother want to suddenly see me? Did he suddenly find religion?"

"He's not the same angry man that you knew, that's for certain," was the answer I received.

"So, he wants to make peace with me before he's put to death?"

There was a mention in the newspaper that he'd be put to death in a couple of weeks if his last appeal for clemency was denied. I hadn't wanted it to happen, but the love I'd once had for Darrell had over transformed the years into embarrassment.

"Yes. And for the sake of everyone involved, come as soon as possible."

"All right. I'll try to get there tomorrow."

Over dinner that night I told Frank about the call.

"I think you should go. If nothing else, at least to say goodbye."

"I'll take the bus after my dialysis session."

"Would you like me to drive you?" Frank asked.

"No, the bus is fine."

"I don't mind, hon. I can juggle my appointments."

"Don't bother. I'd rather go alone."

Frank nodded and the subject was dropped.

***

I was led into a large room with several Plexiglas partitions. The guard seated me in front of one. I noticed a phone on the wall next to me. A door opened and a man in prison garb was led in. I hardly recognized him. His scalp had been shaven, and his arms were completely covered with crude prison tattoos. He was big and muscular.

He nodded, pressed his lips together and picked up a phone. I did the same.

"Long time, sis. You don't look so good."

"Thanks. Did I come here to be insulted?"

A loopy smile formed on his face. A glimpse of the younger brother I once knew flashed before me.

"I'm dying, Darrell. I got some crazy disease that destroyed my kidneys."

"I know."

I looked at him. *How in the world...?*

As if he knew what I was thinking, he said, "Your doctor came to see me."

I was stunned that Dr. Green had made the trip and that my brother spoke to him.

"Says, I'm your *only* hope."

I nodded and gave him a forced smile. "It figures. You're my only living relative."

"I want to help."

I looked at him in wonderment. Had I heard him correctly? Even so, I could feel the tears beginning to fill my eyes.

"I found some peace of mind here, turning to God. Wish I'd done it before I got myself locked up."

"Me, too."

"I'm gonna die in two weeks. I want to do this so's I can face Jesus like a man."

"That's good, Darrell."

"I want to give you my kidneys."

I gasped in surprise.

"The doctor's already had me tested and I'm a match."

"You'd be saving my life, Darrell."

"I know," he said with a huge grin. "Only, the state won't let me."

Was he playing with me? I suddenly felt sick to my stomach. "Why?"

"Cause they're giving me the needle."

"I don't understand," I said, feeling my throat tighten.

"It's simple. The drugs they use will ruin the kidneys. And they won't let me give them to you before my execution because they're afraid I might die and take away their pleasure of killing me."

My heart was shriveling by the second as I listened to Darrell.

"My lawyer is petitioning the parole board as we speak. The doctor came up with a solution..."

I lifted my crestfallen head when I heard those words.

"If we could show something called *just cause*, I might be able to give you one of my kidneys. I'd still have one and be alive so the state could have their justice."

"It's a life and death situation. You'd think that would be enough," I said.

"With the board, you never know."

***

I waited a very long week to find out the parole board's decision. They agreed to allow my brother to have one kidney removed so he could still be executed. Therefore, the following day under heavy guard, he was transferred to County General for the operation. I was prepped to receive it later that same day. The doctor cautioned Frank and me that even though Darrell was a match my body might still reject his kidney. I tried not to dwell on that possibility. The bottom line here was pretty obvious. I didn't want to die. However, at least now I had a possible future.

The surgery went smoothly, and Frank stayed by my side through the most crucial time period afterward. I wanted to be there for Darryl at the end, but I was still recovering from the operation in the hospital. Honestly, I never thought Darrell would do such a wonderful thing and because of it, I'll always be in his debt. May he finally find the true peace in death that had eluded him most of his life. Frank was there at the execution, though, and arranged for proper burial in a nearby cemetery. As soon as I could leave the hospital, I'd visit Darryl's grave. One thing I learned during my ordeal. Life was precious and even in the darkest hour, one should never, ever give up hope.

The End

ICECAPADE

by Candace Gold

- Newcastle, Wyoming—Archaic Law: Couples are banned from having sex while standing inside a walk-in meat freezer

I'm in love with a butcher—plain and simple. Never thought this would happen. Like most girls, I set out to meet and fall in love with a doctor or lawyer. Mama had told me it was just as easy to fall in love with a rich man as it was a poor one. There was one hitch in her advice, though. She neglected to tell me where to find a rich man or how to teach my heart to be more discriminating.

When I first walked into Smith's Meats to buy a pork chop, it was definitely not love at first sight. As Jake Bronson ambled over to wait on me, my eyes were immediately drawn to his apron splattered with dark splotches of dried blood and then the huge, menacingly looking, meat cleaver he was holding in his right hand. It was only on the second glance at this mountain of a man, I noticed his thick blue-black head of hair tumbling down to the back of his shirt collar. It was the kind of hair you wanted to curl your fingers around. His smiling hazel eyes, thin straight nose and full, pillowed lips rounded out a most attractive looking face. Without the props, he was quite an appealing package.

"Can I get you something?" he asked, putting the meat cleaver down on a cutting board.

As he smiled, I noticed he had two dimples to match the sexy deep cleft in his chin, however, I got the distinct feeling he wasn't looking at my face. Was he checking me out as I checking him?

"A nice pork chop, please."

"One?" he asked, looking at me as if I'd suddenly grown a second head.

"Yes. I only need one."

It was for my dinner. I was celebrating the sale of an article I'd written to a magazine. Living alone, I rarely cooked.

"No one buys only one," he replied with an air of authority.

Says who? Anger crept into my voice as I replied, "Well, I do. Now, will you please give me my pork chop?"

He answered me with a shrug, pulled out a tray and selected a chop. However, from the way he ripped off a sheet of freezer paper and slapped the chop down, I knew he was steaming. I watched him deftly wrap it. As he handed it to me, he asked, "Anything else, *Ma'am?*"

"No. That's all, thank you," I replied as I began to walk away, still annoyed with the man's rudeness and roving eyes.

"You know, you shouldn't eat alone," he called after me.

That did it! Who the devil did he think he was? I stormed back over to the counter to confront him. My personal life was just that—personal.

"And what's it to you?" I asked.

He gave me that stupid shrug again. How I hated it when he did that.

"Just figured a pretty gal like you should have company."

"That's none of *your* concern."

"Maybe. There are lots of things I care about," he said, staring at my chest again.

He certainly wasn't winning points with me. *Too bad*, I thought. After all, he was quite a good looking guy. Busy with my own thoughts, I missed the last thing he'd said.

"Well, how do you intend to do it?" he asked.

What the devil was he talking about now? "Do what?"

"Cook the chop?"

Now I looked at him as if he were crazy. Why did he care how I cooked the damn thing? Next, he'll ask me how I intend to chew it. I threw back my head and placed my hands on my hips.

"Put it in a pan and fry it," I answered, defiantly.

Suddenly his face darkened like a winter's sky and his voice, cold and lashing. "Are you nuts, lady? How can you take a beautiful piece of meat and murder it?"

"What do you know? You can cook it better?" I challenged, leaning over the counter.

"You bet, I can," he replied with more than a hint of contempt.

His tone aroused and infuriated me. I wasn't going to let him have the last word. I chortled. "What does a man know about cooking?"

"A great deal...and I can prove it!" His glare met mine.

"Sure, you can," I taunted him.

"You don't believe me? I'll come home with you tonight and show you how to cook pork chops properly," he replied to my challenge.

"Then you'd better bring another to replace this one when you ruin it," I added.

All at once the realization of what had just taken place hit me. I'd just invited a total stranger to my apartment to cook dinner for me. How in the world did I allow it to happen? Before I could open my mouth to switch feet, he sealed the deal.

"I'll be closing in forty minutes. Give me your address," he said handing me a pencil and a small, green order pad to write it down.

I felt as if I'd signed my own death sentence. The way he handled that meat cleaver, he could be a murderer. After all, he *was* a butcher, wasn't he?

I sped home as if I were possessed, not knowing what to do first. Should I straighten the apartment, shower, make certain the oven is working? *Hold it!* I scolded myself. Listen to what you're saying. Just because he's handsome and seemed to be interested in you, you're tripping over your tongue. You're acting like an adolescent. Pull yourself together, girl. He'll be here soon. And for heaven's sake, don't act as if you haven't gone out on a date for ages—no matter how true.

By the time the handsome butcher knocked on my door, I'd been able to clear the old newspapers off the extra kitchen chair and put away the dishes in the drying rack. I would never add good housekeeping to my resume. Unfortunately, it was even further below my cooking skills.

The butcher walked inside carrying a package of meat, a bottle of wine and a single long-stemmed red rose. I was confused. First, he chastises me for the premeditated murder of a pork chop and then he comes waltzing in as if he were going to wine and dine me and… Who the hell *was* this guy?

There was an embarrassed half-smile plastered on the man's face as he said, "Hello…?"

"MaryAnn. My name is MaryAnn Hedges."

The red hue quickly faded from his face and his smile became whole again as he replied, "I'm Jake Bronson."

"Come on in, Jake. Sorry, it's not much," I apologized, suddenly ashamed of my studio apartment with the second-hand furnishings. Unfortunately, big bucks don't come with my job description at the bank.

"It kinda looks like mine," he said walking towards the small wrought–iron kitchen table where he put the meat and wine down.

"I'll take that," I said taking the rose and placing it into a half-filled water glass, making a mental note to invest in a vase.

"If we're gonna eat sometime tonight, I'd better start cooking," Jake said.

"Can I help?"

"You can get me the following stuff: breadcrumbs, salt, pepper, cornstarch, garlic, oil tomatoes—"

"Whoa! Slow down. You lost me."

"Sorry. I'll find the things I need myself. You set the table—or better still—make a salad. You *do* have fresh vegetables in the frig, don't you?"

Luckily, I did. For some reason, I felt like having a salad yesterday and had stopped at the market on the way home from work.

I nodded, feeling good about having done something right. Jake quickly busied himself gathering the ingredients he needed. He looked like he knew his way around a kitchen. This aroused my curiosity as well as something else I couldn't quite define yet.

Ripping apart the lettuce, I asked, "Where did you learn to cook?"

He continued to bread the chops without turning to face me and said, "My mother died when I was thirteen. Being the oldest of four kids and Dad working two jobs, I had no choice."

I wondered what other things he could do as well.

It wasn't long before the kitchen smelled wonderful. A home-cooked meal was another thing I'd not had in ages.

I set the table. There was little room to put anything in addition to the plates, glasses, and silverware. Even so, I put the rose in the center. This space problem never came up before. I usually ate dinner at the sink right out of the pot.

I watched Jake as he began to put everything on platters. He was such an attractive man, one I'd like to get to know better. Okay, it could my loneliness be talking. It had been some time since I'd had a meaningful relationship.

"Have you a corkscrew?" Jake asked interrupting my thoughts.

"Yes. I'll get it," I replied walking towards my so-called junk drawer where I kept miscellaneous items. The only problem was once you took something out; you could never close the drawer again. This time, I was lucky and only struggled a few moments before I succeeded. I handed it to him, and he popped the cork, shooting it clear across the room. We both broke into laughter before I retrieved it.

We began to eat. The man could cook, and I was impressed. All the men I'd known in my life, including my dad, only went into the kitchen to eat. Cooking to them was alien. Only women and wusses cooked.

"Jake, this is delicious. This is by far the best pork chop I've ever eaten."

Jake broke into a huge grin. "You ought to see what else I can do—"

"Shouldn't we wait for the third date?" I replied, trying to repress a smile.

He began to laugh. "I was referring to my special chicken dish."

"Of course, you were."

After breaking the ice, we reached the part where we talked about ourselves and tried to learn as much as we could about each other. I'd rather hear all about him, though. Not having what you'd call a sterling childhood, I tried to forget it ever existed, let alone discuss it. My dad was a gambler who lost his job, the household savings, and insurance. Mom took me and left him, forced to struggle to keep a roof over our heads and food on the table.

Jake stayed until 11:30. We'd had such a good time, we made a real date for the following Saturday. I went to bed wondering if he was the one man put on this earth for me. From what I could see at this point, he certainly met all the criteria.

***

The week blew by. Jake took me to his favorite steak house for dinner. Afterward, we went to play pool. He had brought his own cue stick and knew how to use it.

"My grandfather taught me how to play when I was seven," he said.

"I don't want to ruin your game. I'll watch you play—"

"Don't be silly. It's fun. Come here. I'll show you."

I took the cue and he put his arms around me to guide the shot. Being so close to him, his aftershave intoxicated me, and my skin tingled where he touched me. I wanted to forget the game and lose myself in him.

"It's all in the angles," he was telling me, but I found it so hard to concentrate.

He made it seem so easy. No matter how bad I was, he patiently encouraged me. I was beginning to have fun when his cell phone rang.

He glanced at the caller ID and his smile was quickly replaced by a look of apprehension.

"Gotta take this he said," walking out of earshot.

As I attempted to hit the seven ball into the pocket, I watched him gesture as he spoke. Whoever had called him was not on his Christmas list. The call was quick, and he returned in a soured mood.

"Sorry," he said.

I didn't want to pry, but I was concerned. "Are you okay, Jake?"

"Couldn't be better," he spat. "Let's get out of here. I need some air."

Without another word, he put his cue stick back into its case and we left. He took me home.

As he walked me to my apartment, I asked, "Would you like to come in for coffee or wine?"

He shook his head. "I have to get up early tomorrow and open up."

"Maybe next time."

"Sure," he said, but it felt as if his mind was elsewhere and he was merely brushing me off.

He began to walk away, leaving me disappointed. Then as if he were reading my mind, Jake walked back and kissed me. He had the most kissable lips and the kiss sent me spinning. Still reeling, I heard him say, "I'll call you," before he left.

I chalked up his change in behavior to having to cover another guy's shift. No one likes to ever go in on their day off. I should know. I often had to do it at the bank.

***

Jake and I continued to date, and I had fallen in love with him. In my heart, I knew he was the guy I wanted to share my life with—until I discovered another side of him.

We were having a ball at the State Fair acting like a pair of kids when his cell phone rang. Jake looked upset, reminding me of the night in the pool hall. However, this time, I heard him reply. "Okay, okay, I told you…I'll have the money by next Wednesday."

My stomach knotted. Jake had either borrowed money from a loan shark or worse, lost a bet. I'd had my fill of gamblers and swore I'd never get involved with one.

"What's wrong, Jake?"

"This doesn't concern you."

"Hey, I love you. What kind of future could we have together if you don't trust me?" I asked, half-wanting not to know.

"I bet on the ponies. It was a sure thing."

"My father used to tell my mother the same thing. You know what's definite—?"

"I know. Death and taxes. I knew I shouldn't have told you."

I took his hand. "Listen to me, Jake. Gambling destroyed my family and killed my dad. If you win one bet, you lose three more. Promise me you'll stop," I begged him.

"I don't know if I can," he replied.

"If you don't, I can't be with you."

His eyes pleaded with me to take my words back, but I couldn't.

"I'll help you, Jake, I said. "Only, you've got to swear you'll stop."

He grabbed me by my shoulders and covered my mouth with his before he whispered, "I swear."

I helped Jake raise the money to pay his bookie and he kept his word to stop betting. Had he not, leaving him would have been the most difficult thing I'd ever done.

***

Jake and I were fast asleep when the annoying ringing of his phone awakened us. After a night of lovemaking, I'd welcomed sleep. Groggily, I raised my head to see Jake answer.

"Do you know what time it is?" he growled into the receiver. "So, what? 5:00 am is no time to call anyone. Jerry's always sick. What if I don't want to come in? Okay! I

heard you the first time. I'll be there," he said, slamming the receiver down hard enough to break it.

"What's wrong, Jake?" I asked, rubbing his back.

"Go back to sleep, MaryAnn," he said as he rose from the bed. Just seeing his wickedly beautiful body began to stir my juices.

"Where are you going at this hour?"

"To take a shower. Jerry's called in sick. I've gotta take his damn shift again."

This was the third time this month. We'd made plans to go to a barbecue today at his brother's house. I'd been looking forward to going. Jake turned back. "I'm sorry about the barbecue."

"Not your fault."

"I'll bring home a nice London broil," he replied, probably hoping to appease me.

I rolled over and closed my eyes. I never heard him leave.

***

When I came out of the shower, I noticed the red light on the answering machine blinking. Thinking I'd missed Jake's call, I played back the message.

"Bronson! No more stalling. I want my money today!" the raspy voice of a heavy smoker snarled. "I'm sending Iggy to the store. If you don't have it, I don't have to tell ya what's gonna happen..." This message was followed by a choking laugh before the connection was finally broken.

"Damn you, Jake!" I said aloud. "You promised to stop gambling."

Then it hit me. I had to warn him. I grabbed the phone and called the store. It was busy. I tried his cell number and nearly lost it when it went directly into his voice mail. There was no time to waste. I threw on some sweats and drove to the store, praying I'd get there before this Iggy person. As angry as I was with Jake for breaking his promise and betting again, I couldn't bear to see him hurt by some loan shark's enforcer. I'll never forget how my father looked. I envisioned Iggy to be a gorilla of a man who loved his Louisville slugger more than his own mother.

As I drove, every passing second felt like a hand at my throat tightening its grip,

making each breath more and more difficult. By the time I parked the car and rushed into the store, I was breathless. And so afraid for Jake.

I startled Jake and the elderly woman he was waiting on. They both looked at me as if I were some lunatic. She paid for her meat and left there as quickly as her arthritic legs could carry her, not waiting for her change.

"What's wrong, MaryAnn? You look like you've seen a ghost." Jake said, eyebrows still raised in surprise.

Forcing myself to breathe, I spoke in gasps. "Iggy's on his way here to collect money."

The color drained from Jake's face. "Iggy? How do *you* know?"

"Your loan shark called the apartment. You've been betting again. How could—"

The slamming of a car door interrupted me. Jake came around the counter and grabbed my hand. With me in tow, he headed for the walk-in freezer. Just as the heavy door closed behind us, we heard the bells over the front door tinkle. I prayed it was only a customer.

Jake held a finger to his lips. I watched as he grabbed a broom standing by the door and wedged it into the handle. Then he pushed me further into the room. The overwhelming smell nearly made me retch as I knocked into disgusting animal carcasses hanging from meat hooks. I could swear the pigs were staring at me with their lifeless beady eyes. The sawdust on the floor stuck to the soles of my sneakers. It felt like the Arctic in there and I began to shiver from the cold. Jake put his arm around me. I was miserable, but I knew the alternative was worse.

Suddenly we heard pounding on the door as loud as thunder. Jake drew me closer.

"Bronson! I know you're in there. Come out now and I won't break every bone."

"Nice guy," I whispered.

The lack of color on Jake's face wasn't just from the cold. Nor was the worry in his eyes. He was as frightened as I was.

The pounding grew louder and more intense. Iggy was probably getting frustrated. As he banged on the door and tugged at the latch, he made threats and screamed obscenities. "You're a dead man, Bronson! You hear me? A dead man!"

Now I truly feared for Jake's life. What if Iggy was able to get the door of the freezer open? He didn't sound like the kind of guy who'd listen to reason. An involuntary shiver shook my body.

"I'm so sorry, baby," he whispered.

"Why'd you do it? You promised."

"It was a sure thing. Honest. I swear it."

"Nothing but death and taxes—and Iggy—are sure things."

"But I needed the money."

"What was so important?" I asked him without hiding the anger I felt.

"I...I wanted to buy something," he replied, looking away.

"Nothing could be so important you'd put your life in danger."

"The truth is...I wanted to buy a ring for you."

I looked at him, speechless. Tears began to fill my eyes. "Oh. Jake," I began, but I couldn't speak. He gently touched my face and kissed the top of my head. With tears streaming down my face, I looked up at him. My anger had abated. He did it because of me—because he loved me. I loved him, too. And now I feared I'd lose him because of some creature named Iggy.

He wiped the tears from my face and gave me a smile before he covered my mouth with his. It was a gentle kiss. We kissed again, but this one became more passionate. Soon the beating of our hearts drowned out Iggy. We sank to the floor oblivious to the sawdust covering it. Our passion had become bewitching, allowing us to forget our present surroundings and the danger we were in. All we saw was each other. The articles of clothing separating our newly heated bodies from one another were quickly discarded as we made frantic love amongst the hanging carcasses in the freezer.

We were way too busy defrosting the freezer to notice the pounding had stopped. Only when the door of the freezer was removed from its squeaky hinges, did it get our attention. Suddenly, we looked up and found ourselves surrounded by Jake's boss, Alton Smith, two gawking policemen, and three smirking firemen. I grabbed my jacket in a feeble attempt to cover up. To say I was mortified would be an understatement.

"What the hell are you two doing? The shop is trashed," Smith said, glaring at us with such anger, I quickly froze again. "I'm holding you responsible, Jake."

"I'll make good," Jake said.

"The hell you *will*. Why are you in the freezer in the first place?" Smith asked.

"I'm afraid we're all going to have to take this downtown," one of the policemen said, interrupting.

"What for?" Smith asked. "I'm only pressing charges against that lunatic you have out there."

"I'm afraid *this* is an entirely different issue," the cop answered.

"What issue?" both Smith and Jake asked, nearly in unison.

"I believe they've broken the law, penal code 1148. It concerns fornicating in a freezer."

"You've got to be kidding," Jake said.

"I assure you, sir, I am *not* joking. Now if you and the lady will get dressed..."

"Would you please give us some privacy?" I asked.

The other cop who had remained quiet until now said, "What's there left to see?"

I think Jake's clenched fists and murderous look helped the other men see things differently. After they walked out, we began to dress quickly.

"I don't believe this, Jake."

"And I suppose you think I do?" he snapped.

"It's no use for us to argue. We're in this together."

"I'm sorry, hon. Things haven't been going quite right today."

"You've noticed," I replied, brushing as much sawdust off of me as possible. It was starting to get itchy in places I never thought possible.

"Let's go, you two!" a voice called into the freezer.

"No matter what, MaryAnn, you've got to believe how sorry I am about all this," he said gesturing with his arms.

Remembering the reason why he needed the money in the first place, I softened my tone and gently touched the side of his face. "I know."

He took my hand and we walked out together. No matter what happened next, we'd face it as a team.

***

We were hauled in front of a judge. The nameplate sitting on his huge wooden desk read Thomas A. Poole. The man looked as if he'd been roused from his bed. Thin as a rail, sagging skin the color of sandpaper, the bags under his nearly colorless eyes were more like buckets. His hair, white as freshly fallen snow, stood on ends in places, looking as if it were cut by a buzz saw. He had a scowl on his face and a bulbous nose that reminded me of a well-used road map. A set of hanging jowls completed the picture likening him to a bloodhound. Something told me we were in for it. I prepared for the worst.

Poole waved a long, arthritic-looking, bony finger at the both of us. "Shame on you! You've broken the law. What do you have to say for yourselves?"

"It's my fault, Your Honor—" Jake began to say, but Poole shut him down.

"Who gave you permission to speak—?"

"But Your Honor—" Jake protested.

"It was a rhetorical question, young man. You are to speak *only* when I tell you to."

Oh, boy, I thought. *We've got ourselves a real winner.*

"You are accused of fornicating while standing inside a store's meat freezer. What say ye?"

Neither one of us uttered a sound. The color of the Judge's face began to redden. "I asked you a question," he spat.

"Does that mean you want us to speak?" Jake asked.

"Are you deaf or just plain stupid?" Poole replied.

"We're not guilty, Your Honor," I said.

As Poole's face now took on a purplish hue, I felt the eyes of the two policemen, who had escorted us into court, bore into me. Jake looked at me, eyebrows raised. I put a finger to my lips. I wanted him to trust me. I knew where I was going with this.

"What did you just say, young lady?" Poole asked, fixing his rheumy eyes on me.

I swallowed hard, repeating what I'd just said.

Poole looked so angry I thought the large, throbbing, blue blood vessel on the side of his wizened head would explode. Instead, he banged his gavel a few times. "Are you daft, as well? You were caught with your knickers down and you stand there telling me you're innocent...I should throw the book at both of you."

"Your Honor, Sir, according to the penal code, a couple is banned from having sex while standing. Jake and I...we...were not standing. We were lying on the floor."

"Officer Stewart, how did you find them?" Poole asked.

"On the floor, Your Honor," he said I nearly a whisper.

"Speak up!" Poole demanded.

He repeated his statement. Visible beads of sweat had formed along his high forehead. The Judge looked like he was going to boil him in oil. Instead, Poole made a sound that sounded like a low growl.

"As far as I'm concerned, you two are guilty as sin. Intercourse is intercourse in my book whether you're standing or not. However, in our bleeding, liberal-livered society, some ambulance-chasing moron of a lawyer will get you off. Get out of my court," he said and slammed the gavel down as hard as he could.

Jake hugged me and together we high-tailed it out of there. All we heard as we fled was Poole ordering the two policemen to remain. I had a feeling they both were in big trouble.

"Baby, you were magnificent!" Jake said, kissing me.

"We're not out of the frying pan, yet," I said seeing Anton Smith walking towards us.

"Huh, what do you mean?" he asked.

Before I had a chance to answer, Smith stood before us.

"Look, before you fire me, I intend to work, even overtime, in order to repay you for the damage," Jake said.

Instead of ragging on Jake, the man broke into a huge smile and clapped him on the back. Now I was certain the entire world had gone mad.

"You're not angry?" Jake asked, obviously just as bewildered as I was.

"Of course not," Smith replied.

"I don't understand," Jake replied, definitely wondering about his sudden change of heart.

"Thanks to your little run-in with your loan shark, I can now renovate. The insurance company has agreed to pay for everything. You're off the hook, man."

Now if only Jake could get squared away with the loan shark. A ray of hope entered my thoughts. If only Iggy was promised a deal and ratted out his boss... Whatever, it didn't matter. Jake wasn't alone in this. We'd find some way to raise the money together. Afterward, I'd delete the loan shark's number from Jake's cell phone, permanently.

We walked out of the courthouse arm-in-arm, a great deal happier than when we first entered.

"Hungry?" Jake asked.

"Starved," was my reply.

"I know just the thing," he said pulling me towards the hotdog stand. "Tell the man what you'd like."

I ordered two dogs with everything on them. Jake got the same. We sat together on a bench biting into oozing hot dogs, getting more mustard and chili on our faces than in our mouths. To tell the truth, I was having the time of my life. After they were completely devoured and we'd made an attempt to clean ourselves up, Jake reached into his pocket and pulled out a small jewelry box. He handed it to me and said, "Open it."

My hands trembled. Inside I found a beautiful diamond ring.

"MaryAnn Hedges, will you marry me?"

"You know I will," I replied as he slipped the ring on my finger.

"I guess it was just one of those *sure* things," he said, grinning.

Then he took me in his arms, and we kissed. We were interrupted by a cranky voice. "You two are incorrigible. I should have slapped both your asses in jail when I had the chance." The judge was standing there before us shaking his head.

THE END

Courted by a Con-Man
Candace Gold

Carolyn Wilkerson took stock of her life one day in late September as she walked through a lovely little park several blocks away from the real estate firm that she owned. Watching the leaves start to change color, she knew that her life had to change before she withered and was left old and alone. As winter drew near with the coming holidays, she knew she'd become melancholy and bring on the self-pity she experienced over her two failed marriages that affected her both physically and mentally. However, enough time had gone by buffering her past. She had to grab the reins of life and look toward the future and help mold it as much as humanly possible.

If Carolyn could sum up her present existence in one word, it would be loneliness. And she was tired of coming home to an empty apartment day after day. With the terms of her lease, she couldn't even own a cat. Moving wouldn't help. She didn't want a pet. Nor did she need one. What she needed was a companion, a confidant, and a lover. It was time.

Carolyn had decided she was ready to take a chance again and date. And if the right person happened to come along, allow herself to fall in love. She knew that Prince Charmings didn't ride by on trusty steeds. Nor did it rain men as a pop song had insinuated. Carolyn realized that she had to play an active part in finding her Mr. Right.

Kirsten Blaine, Carolyn's closest friend, confidant, and work associate was also single. With blond hair and blue eyes, she could pass for Carolyn's sister. And like Carolyn, Kirsten was in her forties. Tired of the dating rat-race consisting of blind dates and casual meetings at social gatherings and bars, she turned to online dating sites. One site, in particular, had decent candidates and she even dated several men at least once. She suggested that Carolyn try the sight. After all, nothing gained, nothing lost, right?

Carolyn took Kirsten's advice and checked out the dating e-site. As she scrolled through the headshots of the men, she selected several, jotting down their specifics. Looking over her selections, she chose two and emailed her profile with a recent picture.

In her email inbox the following day she found responses from both men. The quick turnaround surprised Carolyn. She read and reread their replies carefully. In the back of her mind was the realization that whatever the men said, as well as their photos, could all be embellished. Just because she'd been honest didn't mean others would as well.

Carolyn compared the information from both men and opted to meet the taller of the two, James Delaney, who claimed he was 6'4". From the headshot in the original post, she could see he possessed a full head of black hair and deep blue eyes. An attractive man, James described himself as a man who traveled often because of his job as a fire protection engineer who designed sprinkler systems for new buildings and was lonely and looking for companionship. If he met the right woman, he was willing to travel less and settle down.

Carolyn corresponded with James for nearly a week before making a date to meet. She found his emails warm and witty. If he was as lonely as she, perhaps they'd click. Carolyn was ready to take the big step and have lunch with him, something she feared would never happen following her traumatic divorces. She feared she just brought out the worst in men.

Her first husband was verbally abusive and often cheated on her. When Carolyn finally got the courage to divorce him, he fought her at every turn. It was her second husband and consequent divorce that nearly destroyed her. It was like living with Dr. Jekyll and Mr. Hyde. He turned out to be a psychopath and met his demise by running his car off the road into a ravine. Though it was ruled an accident and not a suicide, she felt she'd had played a role in his accident by asking for a divorce.

However, all that was behind her now. She had to move on with her life after wasting too much of it on drama caused by her exes. No one ever knew what lie ahead any more than Carolyn did, but she could make the best of it and that was exactly what she intended to do.

James Delaney's emails were nearly poetic. His use of words and how he turned them into phrases resonated with Carolyn and she enjoyed corresponding with him. Could he be the one to give her life new meaning? She intended to find out.

Carolyn had her first lunch date with James Delaney a week later. They met at a small Mexican restaurant several blocks from her real estate office. He was already there sitting at a small round table when she walked in. She knew exactly who he was because of his picture. At least he didn't attempt to embellish his photo. A mental check was drawn in the pro column of her mind. The smile on his handsome suntanned face was electric.

Dressed casually in an expensive-looking polo shirt and slacks, James stood, and she took him all in, initially likening him to a Greek god rising from the sea. He was a big man, tall and broad, muscular in the chest and narrow in the waist. *So far so good*, Carolyn thought as James extended his hand to shake hers.

They both sat down as the waitress approached the table and handed them menus. "What would you like to drink?"

Both asked for coffee which was brought quickly. "I'll be back to take your order."

James smiled. "You're more beautiful than your photo."

Carolyn blushed. "Thank you. I can say the same about you." Then realizing what she'd said, stammered, "I don't mean pretty, but handsome, of course."

James chuckled at her gaffe in a good-natured way. "This is my first foray into online dating, as well."

"Perhaps we can stumble along the bumpy road together," Carolyn suggested.

"That's a good idea. I already know you're honest, as well as modest."

"Any relationship needs honesty for a strong foundation."

James added his take on the subject. "Words to live by." Then noticing the waitress preparing to return to their table to take their order, said, "We'd better decide on what we're eating."

Several minutes passed as Carolyn and James scanned the menu. They looked up to see the waitress standing by their table.

"Ready to order?" the tired-looking woman asked, poised to write down their choices.

Carolyn nodded and ordered a club sandwich. James ordered the same and the waitress put in their order before returning to refill their coffee cups. Once the waitress left, their conversation began in earnest. Carolyn wanted to learn more about the handsome man who claimed he traveled a great deal because of his job, so she asked what a fire protection engineer actually did. In her mind, in particular, she envisioned firefighters and the like.

James smiled. "Not many people truly know what kind of work I do thinking that I act in some capacity as a fireman. That couldn't be the furthest from the truth. Actually, I design water sprinkler systems for new building construction. It's definitely challenging work but knowing that what I did potentially saved lives had its own rewards."

Carolyn was clinging on to every word. He sounded so passionate about his profession. It was so refreshing to hear a guy speak so highly and enjoy his occupation. "It's refreshing to hear someone enjoy their job."

"It does seem to have a drawback, though."

"What might that be?" Carolyn asked.

"It prevents me from finding the right woman with whom to settle down since I'm away from home a great deal for weeks and even months at a time."

"Would that matter if a woman truly loved you? After all, many women are married to soldiers who go off to serve in other countries around the world. Just think of the happiness when he returns," Carolyn said.

Shrugging, James said, "You know, I never looked at it from that perspective."

"Perhaps you might not have met the right woman to share the rest of your life with. Honestly, I've always thought there was a right man for every woman. That belief was nearly extinguished by my failed marriages. It caused me to wall up myself and hide how I felt away. I feared to put my toe back in the water and to get hurt."

Carolyn couldn't believe she'd opened up so widely to James, but his reaching over to place his hand on hers reassured her that it was okay. "We all do the same thing. No one wants to get hurt, Carolyn." He smiled as he patted her hand gently.

His smile made her smile. They continued their conversation even after their sandwiches arrived. Carolyn got good vibes from this guy. He was easy to be and talk with. She wondered if James could be the real deal. And was she truly ready to try again? Or was all this just her loneliness talking? The one thing that she did know was that if she didn't see James again, she'd never know.

Toward the end of their meal, James wiped his mouth with his napkin and said, "I truly enjoyed your company today, Carolyn and would like to take the next step with you."

"Which is?" she asked, trying not to sound too eager.

"Dinner, of course. I'd like to take you to a fantastic restaurant I came across by accident."

"That sounds nice. Just tell me where and when," she replied.

"How's about next Saturday at 6:00? I'll pick you up at your place if you like."

Though Carolyn felt it would be okay to let James know where she lived, someone once told her to continue to meet the man until you were certain. She heeded these words. Better to be safe than sorry.

"No, James. It would be easier for me if I just met you there," she replied, figuring that she really wasn't lying. It would be easier on her psyche. No fear.

James seemed perceptive enough to read between the lines and smiled. "I understand." Then he gave her the name and address of the restaurant including the cross streets.

They continued talking a little while longer before saying goodbye. James kissed Carolyn on the cheek. and they parted. As Carolyn walked away, she had a distinct feeling that if she turned around, she'd see James standing there watching her. She liked the fact that he might be looking after her and hoped it meant he truly was interested in her. Then again, despite her eagerness, remnants of her dark paranoia centering around relationships still remained. She only hoped that James was the real deal.

During the week, Carolyn thought a great deal about James. They spoke several times on the phone and with each phone call, she felt more at ease. He was sweet and caring—definitely the kind of guy she was looking for. James seemed to know what to say to make her feel better and it apparently showed.

At work, Kirsten asked, "Did you get laid last night?"

"No! I only just met the guy, and it was for lunch."

"Well, you certainly look happy. Tell me about him."

"He's nice and knows how to treat a woman. And very old school, because he wants to take things slowly," Carolyn said.

"Good. After what you've been through, you deserve happiness."

"I really like this guy, Kirsten. He so down to earth."

"Those are great traits, but just remember not to rush into anything."

Their conversation was interrupted by a patron who'd just walked in. Kirsten steered the man to her desk.

***

On Saturday Carolyn spent hours getting ready for her date with James. Like a teenager, she wanted her hair and dress to be perfect. She hadn't been so upbeat about going out with a guy in such a long time.

James met Carolyn at an upscale restaurant not too far from her realty office. She'd never eaten there but knew that it was top-notch. It would seem that James had wanted to impress her, too.

She'd come early and was surprised to see James standing in front of the restaurant looking handsome in a blue sports jacket and beige slacks. His shirt was off white, and his tie was red. His face broke into a wide smile as he took in her black dress and matching heels. Her blonde hair had been swept up in a French knot to give her an air of sophistication.

"You look splendid," James said as Carolyn reached him. "I believe our table is available, so let's go inside," he said as he put his arm around her and guided her to the door.

From the moment they sat down and both she and James had selected the house prime rib special to the last drop of champagne had been drunk, all Carolyn saw was James. He loomed large and filled her world with romance and thoughts of a rosy future. And that surprised her after she'd been so guarded for so long.

As they left the restaurant, James turned to kiss Carolyn goodnight. It was a soft kiss, but it was enough to stoke the budding embers inside of her. Perhaps it was the champagne that helped mellow Carolyn and the fact she'd not been with a man for so long, that caused her to cast her fate to the wind and ask James if he'd like to follow her home for a nightcap.

"I'd love to, Carolyn, but I don't want you to regret it tomorrow."

Carolyn smiled. "I don't think that will happen."

James gently cupped her chin and gently kissed her. "I'm glad to hear that," and kissed her more fervently this time.

He followed her to her car and then went to his own. Carolyn waited for him to reach the exit of the parking lot before she turned on to the street. All the way home, she drove as if she were floating on a cloud. She hadn't felt this wonderful about a guy in a long time and began to fanaticize how it would be like to make love with James. Of course, she constantly looked in her rearview mirror to make certain the dark gray Land Rover was still behind her.

Carolyn took out her front door key and James took it from her hand and opened the door for her. He followed her inside her apartment. They got as far as half-way down the central hall before he took her in his arms and kissed her with the passion she so sorely missed. That kiss led to another and they danced their way into her bedroom. Slowly, they undressed one another, stealing kisses between each item of clothing. Finally, they fell back onto the bed. James balanced himself on an elbow and looked dreamily into Carolyn's eyes. "You're so beautiful," he said, before nuzzling her neck.

Carolyn's insides were beginning to melt into liquid fire as his lips began to slowly move down her neck to her breasts. With his hands exploring the rest of her, she felt something akin to an electric shock scorching her body. She was fully aware of the hardness of his manhood brushing against her thigh and shifted her body so that she could guide it inside herself. She gasped in pleasure as he filled her. When they began to move in unison, the intensity increased to the point where she cried out.

It had been quite a while since Caroline had experienced such sexual pleasure that even after a short period of cuddling together, she was more than ready to be made love to again when James reached for her. It would appear that James was indeed the guy she'd hoped to meet. He possessed everything she desired in a man. The fact that she was rushing headfirst into a relationship and not taking it slowly didn't bother her. She was so that into James that she stifled the tiny voice of caution in the back of her head, allowing him into her life.

In the weeks and then months ahead, James spent a great deal of time at Carolyn's place. He still maintained his own condo and hadn't gone on any business trips for nearly five months. It took another two months before he began to hint at taking the next step in their relationship. Carolyn merely figured James meant moving in together, only she was wrong.

"I'm a traditional kind of guy. I just don't want to live with you like a roommate. I want the whole ball of wax because I know you're the one woman I want to spend the rest of my life with."

After that heartfelt declaration, they began to discuss marriage. Kirsten thought Carolyn was rushing into something so permanent so soon and tried to slow her down. "If it's true love and not just a passing bout of lust, time won't hurt the relationship. Trust me."

Only Carolyn was so smitten with James that Kirsten's words didn't penetrate the romantic haze that enveloped her. She and James began to plan their nuptials in earnest.

Carolyn had experienced the big wedding scene already and didn't care to go through all that planning again. James didn't care whether or not they had a big affair. To him, it was the ends that justified the means. The journey a couple took to stand in front of a minister was meaningless. It was taking the vows that counted. All this planning had to be put on hold anyway since he had taken a job to draw up fire safety plans for a medical building in Tacoma.

The week that James was away proved to be a lonely one for Carolyn. In an attempt to keep her mind busy, she spent more time at the office. Even emerging herself in her business didn't succeed in capturing her thoughts that were revolving around James. In fact, she could hardly wait for Sunday morning so she could greet him at the airport.

James was famished having had nothing but coffee to eat on the plane, so Carolyn drove to a diner where he could have something to eat. He looked tired and Carolyn wondered if he'd gotten any sleep. He seemed to sense she was thinking about him and interrupted her thoughts. "I worked on the initial plans most of the day and half the night. Then I made certain that they'd be implemented correctly. No use planning when the execution ended up sucking."

"I thought you looked tired. Well, I'll make certain you get adequate sleep."

James grinned and reached across the table to pat her hand. "No worries. I'll be fine now that I'm back with you."

Carolyn melted inside. He always seemed to know the right things to say. She was so glad that they found one another. They finished their breakfast and she dropped James off at his place and drove to the real estate office. Kirsten was finishing up with a couple just as Carolyn walked through the door.

"James is home?" Kirsten asked after the couple left.

"Yup. He's tired but good."

"Okay. Just wondering," Kirsten replied and then launched into business talk.

Carolyn stayed in the office until 4:00. She couldn't wait to be with James who promised to be at her place by six. While he was gone, she had a great deal of time to think about their relationship and had come to a decision. It would be fine to continue the way they were with James maintaining a place of his own, but what was the point? When he wasn't traveling, he was at her place nearly every night. And since James claimed to be old-fashioned enough not to want to live together and preferred marriage, she'd say yes if and when he asked her again.

They'd have a unique marriage. With James traveling because of his job, they wouldn't smother one another or give their love the chance to grow stale. With the business trips he took, they'd have time apart and be able to rekindle their love every time he returned home and keep their marriage strong. After her two failed marriages, Carolyn found this quite appealing. Therefore, when the topic of taking the next step in their relationship came up again several weeks later, Carolyn said yes.

Without telling a soul, Carolyn and James flew to Las Vegas and got married. She didn't want a big wedding and neither did he. When she returned home and told Kirsten, Carolyn was surprised by the reaction of her friend and work associate.

"Really? You just plunged headfirst into another marriage. How long do you know this guy?"

"It's not how long, but how well you know a person that counts," was Carolyn's reply.

To that, she got a raised eyebrow from Kirsten. Carolyn knew Kirsten didn't approve but questioned why. Couldn't Kirsten see how happy James made her? And wasn't that the bottom line here?

Only Kirsten didn't let the discussion end there. "Do yourself a favor before the ink dries on the license. Check into his past. Right now, you only know what he's told you. Hopefully, you'll discover only good things, but at least you'll know. Just saying..."

Carolyn did try to go online to find out more about James but couldn't find much. Kirsten had stoked her curiosity. He'd mentioned that he was a fire protection engineer. Did he work for himself as a consultant or for an established company? Had he told her which? No matter how hard she tried, she couldn't remember. Now, how could she just come out and ask without sounding nosy and possibly ruffling feathers? Perhaps when he went on another business trip, she'll be able to find out more.

Two weeks later, James announced that he'd be going on a business trip. That night James was extra romantic, which appeared to be a pattern whenever he was leaving. As he made love to her, Carolyn's mind was on how little she knew James and caused her to be somewhat detached. James being his perceptive self, noticed.

"Carolyn, what's wrong?"

She sighed. "I know we've talked about this, but I hate to see you go. I get so lonely when you're gone."

James tried to soothe her. "It will only be a few days this time."

"Where will you be going this time?"

"A new factory is in construction in Atlanta."

"Where will you be staying in case, I need to reach you?"

"Call my cell," James replied.

Carolyn noticed that he purposely didn't tell her the hotel he was staying at. So, she said, but knowing where you'll be staying, I'll feel closer to you."

James narrowed his eyes. She'd touched a nerve, though she couldn't imagine why. What did he have to hide?

"If knowing will make you feel better, I'll be at the Mariner. I'll leave the number for you."

Carolyn backed off and didn't mention a thing about his trip again.

***

James left in the morning for Atlanta, driving to the airport himself. The telephone number for the Mariner was placed by the landline.

Carolyn went to the office and immersed herself in paperwork. Kirsten and Charles were helping customers. Business was good. She had James who loved her. So why was she suddenly questioning things?

James called late afternoon. Just hearing his voice perked Carolyn up. She was acting foolishly by poking into things that didn't matter. All she should care about was the here and now and look to the future. That was her intention until her brother Carl called that same night.

Carl was several years older than Carolyn and lived in New York with his wife, Anna, and three kids. He could never understand how she could live in Arizona with all that frigging heat. Since he hadn't heard from Carolyn in several weeks, he'd texted her. When he hadn't received any replies, he thought it odd and called her.

"It's about time I got ahold of you, Carolyn."

"Why? Have you called before and not gotten an answer?"

"No. Just sent some texts."

"Never saw them, Carl."

"That's odd. Did you lose your phone?"

"No. I'll check and make sure the texting function's okay. So, is everything okay in New York?"

She could imagine the broad smile on her brother's face as he said, "Anna and the kids are fine. How are things in your life?"

"I got married again—"

"And you didn't think us important enough to know?"

"It was a spur of the moment thing and I should have called. My bad."

"Who is he? Tell me about him."

"Carl, you're going to love him. He's romantic and kind."

"If he's good to you and not crazy, I'm sure I will."

"Bring the family out here on vacation. You know how much I'd love to see you all," Carolyn said.

"You know, you can come out here as well."

"True enough, but business is good, and I need to see that it continues to be so."

They talked a little longer before saying goodbye. When the conversation ended, Carolyn thumbed through all her messages. She didn't see any from her brother and wondered why.

The next day at work was a busy one. Carolyn and Kirsten didn't have a moment to talk so they went out for some Mexican food so they could touch base. Talk concerning the business talk took center stage and after that topic was exhausted, Carolyn mentioned she'd heard from her brother. She also told Kirsten about the missing messages.

"Perhaps you inadvertently erased them, Carolyn. It happens. Sometimes, I quickly thumb through mine and erase them in bulk," Kirsten said.

"I don't recall erasing any, but anything's possible."

"Or, perhaps someone else erased them," Kirsten added.

Those words hung in the air like dark thunder clouds.

"No one else uses my phone," Carolyn said.

"Uh-huh."

Realizing that her friend was hinting at James, Carolyn changed the subject. She didn't want even to think that might be the case. Only Kirsten wasn't buying it.

"My vibes tell me that James is too good to be true. There I said it."

"Are you certain it's not jealousy that's prompting your vibes?"

"Really? I'm not one iota jealous. I merely care about you, Carolyn."

Carolyn signaled the waiter for the check. "Let's call it a night before things are said that might be regretted."

Kirsten, realizing that Carolyn wasn't buying what she was trying to tell her. She certainly hadn't heeded any of her advice up until this point, having already plunged into a hasty marriage. Perhaps, it would be more prudent of her to back off until she had proof to give her.

***

James returned home with a beautiful bracelet for Carolyn which he presented during an intimate dinner at a quiet upscale restaurant. Following their meal, they went back home and made slow, sweet love. *Things were fine. Why look for problems? Kirsten was so wrong about James.*

Only, Kirsten's concern had caused her to contact Joe Heisman, the investigator the firm used to check out dubious clients. They met for coffee out of the office and she laid out her reasons for contacting him.

"Everyone had a past. When they don't, they're hiding something," she concluded.

"It shouldn't take me longer than a few days. I'll call you and we'll meet here with what I find out," Joe said.

They shook hands and each went their separate ways.

Joe called Kirsten two days later. They met at the same coffee shop as before and they ordered coffee. After they sat down and got past the customary chit-chat, he handed her a manila envelope. Kirsten pulled out the report and paled momentarily while she read it. Then she looked up at Joe and thanked him as she handed him the check.

"Keep it," he said. I like Carolyn. This one's on me."

***

Kirsten now had the proof she needed to present to Carolyn. Her vibes about James had been correct. The only problem was where and when to tell her. With James home, Carolyn had been coming to work late and leaving early. Sometimes she even took long lunches. She was so smitten with James that even if Kirsten showed her the info she'd received, Carolyn would never believe a word of it.

The days became weeks and still, the report remained locked in Kirsten's desk drawer. Then one afternoon Kirsten received a phone call from Carolyn's brother, Carl.

"Hi, Kirsten, this Carl, Carolyn's brother. I'm so glad you answered. I've been trying to get in touch with Carolyn, but she hasn't replied to any of my messages or calls."

"Again? If I remember correctly, this happened once before, right?"

"Yes. When I finally got a hold of her, she claimed she never received them."

"Carl, I believe that her husband, James erased them."

"Why on earth would he do that?" Carl said, sounding exasperated.

"Because I believe he's trying to take control of every aspect of her life. He's a sociopath."

Dear God! How did my sister hook up with another crazy guy? What is she a magnet for the misbegotten?"

"I thought something was off with the guy and hired an investigator. It's as bad as I thought, but I haven't shown the report to Carolyn as of yet. She wouldn't believe me just the same."

"We have to do something. I mean we can't just let the guy hurt her. Maybe we should go to the police," Carl suggested.

"And tell them what? The guy hasn't done anything to hurt Carolyn and she's in love with him. There's nothing that the police can do until a crime is committed."

"Shit!"

"Look, I'm here and I have my eyes wide open. If I see a good time, I'll show Carolyn that report."

"All right, but please keep me posted. I don't like being so far away."

"I will, Carl, I promise."

***

At work, the following day, it was quiet in the office and Charles had taken the day off to take care of personal things. Kirsten decided to take this opportunity to show Carolyn the results of the investigation on James. She realized it was now or never and this really couldn't wait.

Kirsten poured two cups of coffee and brought one over to Carolyn's desk. Carolyn looked up and thanked her.

"By the way, your brother called me."

"Why? Why didn't he call me?" Carolyn asked, looking perplexed.

"He said he tried a number of times and left messages—"

"Oh, no..."

"What?" Kirsten asked.

"I never received any of them...again."

"They had to be erased, Carolyn, and there's only one person who could have done that. You and I both know that."

Carolyn covered her face with both hands and began to sob.

"I don't want to be the bearer of bad news, but there's something that I must show you. It will explain everything," Kirsten said.

Carolyn stopped crying and watched as her associate carried over a manila envelope and handed it to her. With shaking hands, Carolyn removed the sheets of paper and began to read. Tears flowed down her cheeks. She knew her investigator was thorough and never left any stone unturned. Nor did he embellish. To him, the truth was exactly that, nothing more. Besides, he had no reason to be biased. He didn't even know James. She couldn't dispute any part of the report since all she knew about James was what he'd told her. According to what she'd read, all of that info was fabricated and if that was the case, did that include his falling in love with her? Was it all an act? His motivation could be her money. There was nothing else.

In the files, there were too many upturned stones that revealed red flags. There was no way that she could ignore what she was reading, though she felt an overwhelming desire to ignore the veracity of the information. Only, deep in her heart, Carolyn knew she couldn't deny what was in the report. And what she read, scared the hell out of her.

The man she married was a sociopath. James was a romantic and suave con man whose wives, and there had been at least four before her, had met dubious ends. If he'd ever received a degree in fire protection, it had been in prison where he served time for arson and assault. If he was a serial killer, how much time did she have left? Then she remembered having questioned him on his last trip. Did that steal precious time away?

Carolyn realized she had to act quickly. Who could tell what James might have in store for her? However, she didn't want to tell him of her desire for a divorce until all her ducks were in a row.

She looked up and saw that Kirsten was watching her, probably wondering what conclusion she'd come to.

"Okay, Kirsten, you've convinced me," Carolyn said walking toward her associate's desk.

"I'm sorry it went this way, but I knew something was off about James. And everything happened way too quickly. Because I care about you, I had to know he was on the level. Only, when I checked his credit, I found no credible history. I had a funny feeling he went by more than one name. That's why I had him investigated fully."

Carolyn hugged her friend. "Thank you for your concern. I know I wasn't too pleased about it."

"Coming to the realization that James is dangerous is the easy part. What comes next will not be," Kirsten replied.

"I know. And I have a feeling I'm going to need your help."

"Anything I can do to help, Carolyn, I'll do. You know that."

The look of determination on Kirsten's face hammered that fact home. She'd always been a good friend and would continue to be one.

When Carolyn came home that night, James informed her he'd be traveling to Colorado for the next several days. During that time while he was away doing God only knew what, Carolyn started divorce proceedings. Her lawyer was doing everything in her power to expedite the process. At the same time, Carolyn changed her will making her brother the sole beneficiary. No matter what happened, she was glad that James would not profit from her death.

***

James came home from Colorado earlier than he said he would and was already cooking dinner when Carolyn walked in after work. Seeing him at the stove stirring sauce turned her insides over. If the sight of him made her sick, she wondered how the hell she was going to make love with him that night? She didn't want him to find out about the divorce until it was time for him to sign. He was dangerous and things could easily go sideways.

He put the spoon down and went to her. She tried to put a smile on her face and some warmth in her kiss. Pushing her away he said, "You look tired. Working hard?"

She sighed heavily. "It's been busy. You're home earlier than I expected you. I would have picked you up at the airport," she lied.

"No worries. It was an easy job without any unexpected problems."

"Do you want me to take over the prep for dinner?"

"Absolutely not. Kick-off your shoes and relax. I got everything under control," he said.

Except for my heart. Carolyn felt it slamming against her chest and needed to get it to slow down. She needed to get out of there. "I'm going upstairs to change. Be right back."

"Don't take too long," James replied. "Dinner's almost ready."

When Carolyn had come back downstairs, James was putting the spaghetti and sauce on the table. He'd already poured two glasses of wine. She opened the refrigerator and got the butter for the Italian bread and the dressing bottle for the salad. Then she sat down willing herself to eat.

"This is lovely, James."

"I aim to please, ma'am."

Carolyn gave James a forced smile. She couldn't believe how quickly her feelings had changed toward him. The very sight of him made her want to throw up. With her insides churning, the possibility was actually real.

After dinner, James helped her clear the table and do the dishes. It was obvious that he wanted to get her into bed as soon as possible. This had been his schtick whenever he returned home from his trips. She had to give an Oscar-worthy performance or else she'd be telling him something was wrong. Her mind began to scramble on some excuse that would explain her unenthusiastic lovemaking when James took her hand and led her upstairs.

"Your hands are cold," he said as they climbed the stairs. "Are you feeling well?"

Bingo! An excuse! "I may be coming down with something. Perhaps I should sleep on the couch tonight."

"Nonsense! I'm healthy as a horse. Nothing can keep me away from my beautiful wife who I missed the past few days."

Shit! "Making you sick would add to my guilt and I don't need any more guilt."

He squeezed her hand in order to reassure her, she suspected, as her mind frantically searched for another excuse. Then again, too many excuses might signal something was off, too.

They undressed and got into bed. James reached for Carolyn and she slid into his arms. Her body began to tremble, but she tried to stop it. He had to believe she was cold and not afraid. She had to prevent things from going sideways. Anything could trigger him.

"Cold?" he said holding her tighter. "I'll get you warm quick enough."

James kissed her and she had to forcibly control her gag reflex. His mouth slid down her body. *Come on muscle memory*, she commanded her body, *don't reveal how I truly feel.*

Move your hands! Run them through his hair. Show him you want this.

James spread her legs and pushed inside. Carolyn tried to keep her body moving in sync with his. It was a tough thing to do when all she wanted to do was scratch his eyes out. Where had all these violent thoughts come from?

When James climaxed, she thought all her worries were over. Only, instead of lying back down beside her, he leaned on one elbow and asked, "What has got you so preoccupied that you can't even make love to your husband?"

"It's nothing, really."

"Oh, but it is, Carolyn. You weren't even happy to see me," James replied, his words chilling her blood.

"Yes, I was. I always miss you so much when you go away," she said.

He cocked his head. "Something happened while I was away. Did you meet another man?"

"No, of course not!"

"Then it has to concern me."

"As much as I care for you James, there are other things I need to worry about," she said, noticing he was inferring that it's always all about him.

"Such as?" His words were icy.

"Things at the agency were hectic these past few days—"

"Wanna try again? The look on your face gave you away, Carolyn."

She tried to laugh that off. "Why are you reading into my look of surprise?"

"Really? You're going to stick with that story?" he said, narrowing his eyes.

"It's the truth and nothing more."

She'd barely finished saying that when he grabbed both sides of her face with his hand and squeezed hard, drawing tears.

"You're lying."

Carolyn tried to shake her head no, but his grip was strong. She attempted to pull his hands away but failed. Fear had permeated every pore of her body. She feared he was going to kill her right there and then. Then he released her face and she fell back onto her pillow. Her cheeks still smarted as if he were still squeezing. She had to get him to leave.

She got out of bed and grabbed her robe.

He growled, "Where are you going?"

"Away from you," she said and went down the steps for her cell phone.

By the time, he'd reached her, she was holding her phone. "I'm calling the police."

"Put the phone down. I don't know what came over me. I'm sorry. The thought of you not loving me anymore drove me crazy."

"You inferred it all. No one hurts me. That's a deal-breaker. Pack your bags and get the hell out of my apartment. Or I will call 911. Your choice," she said, though she was keeping it together by a thread.

Carolyn backed into the kitchen and grabbed a knife for protection. James obviously realized he couldn't change her mind and went back upstairs. When he did, she called 911 and explained her situation. There was no way that she would trust James. By the time he came back downstairs dressed, he was carrying a suitcase. The police greeted him at the door. Carolyn didn't care what they did with him. A female cop with short brown hair and dark brown eyes stayed to speak to her.

"The fingerprints on your face tell quite a story. Did he hurt you anyplace else?"

"No. I'm fine," Carolyn said. "I'm relieved he's gone."

"You'll want to get a writ of protection—though a lot of good it does," the officer said. "Are you certain you don't want to go to the hospital?"

"No." Pointing to her face, "This is the only damage."

"Tomorrow when you are feeling better, stop by the station and make a formal complaint," the officer said and wished Carolyn goodnight.

Carolyn called Kirsten, who happened to be out on a date. After hearing what had happened, she gave Carolyn the garage door code and told her to let herself in. Since her date was a bust, Kirsten told her she'd be home sooner than later.

It was decided that until the locks had been changed, Carolyn would be staying with Kirsten. Carolyn's lawyer got her the restraining order and sent the divorce papers out. Unfortunately, no one knew where James was staying to serve him. Carolyn knew he'd show up again and the prospect scared her. She left a message on James's phone telling him that she was leaving his things in boxes by her front door. If he wanted them, they would be there, but for only a day or so. After that, they'd be in the dumpster.

*****

Carl Strand looked at his watch again wishing that the damn plane would take off, already. There seemed to be a minor problem that needed the attention of some mucky-mucky on the tech food chain. He was heading to Arizona to confront his sister. After speaking to Kirsten and learning the highlights of her charming psycho husband, if she didn't listen to reason, he'd strangle her himself. How was it possible for such a smart woman to marry one loser after another? When it came to men, Carolyn apparently had no common sense. This one, though, scared the hell out of him.

He glanced at his watch again and sighed.

*****

Carolyn realized that she must have poked the bear because when she left her apartment, she saw that James had taken his things, but she found two of her car's tires had been slashed. She looked around quickly but spied neither James nor his car.

Back inside her apartment, she made three phone calls. The first was to the police to report the crime and let them know she wouldn't be in to give a statement until later. The next call was to her insurance company and they recommended a tire place that would change out the tires and even rotate them for her. *What a bargain*, she mused. The last call was to Kirsten to tell her she'd be late to work.

"What's wrong, Carolyn? You sound exasperated."

"James came by to pick up his things and slashed two of my tires. I think he's a tad pissed."

"Ya, think?"

"I'll call an Uber after I take care of my car. The company suggested by my insurance company does house calls and I don't need to be here when they come."

"Okay, Carolyn. Give me a buzz when you're on the way."

Carolyn smiled at the thoughtfulness of her friend. "I will. See you later."

***

Walking out to Kirsten's car after work, Carolyn got a chilling feeling down her spine that they were being watched. Damn, James, he was making her paranoid. If he continued, he would make her as crazy as he. They reached the car.

"There's an ad stuck under the wiper," Carolyn said, going to retrieve it. Her face paled as she read what was written on the page. *You're going to be sorry. Next time mind your own business.*

"What does it say, Carolyn? It's from *him*, isn't it?"

Carolyn got into the car and locked her door. She handed Kirsten the note. Kirsten bit down on her bottom lip as she read it. "Guess we're both in the doghouse."

"Not funny. Should we tell the police?"

Kirsten thought a moment. "We have no tangible proof that James left the note." Then, looking up at the poles and buildings around them, added, "Unless... a camera caught him doing it."

"Just thinking about James leaving that on your car gives me the chills. He could be out there somewhere watching us."

"Come on, Carolyn, let's get the hell out of here."

"Do you want to get a take-out pizza for dinner or go to a restaurant. No matter what, we've got to eat."

"You're right. Let's have some dinner and relax. We're letting James into our heads," Kirsten replied.

The two women ended up going to a sports bar that served great burgers. Both ordered the place's signature burger with onion rings. Not wanting to bring up James in any capacity, they talked about the new rental brochures that came in the mail from yet another apartment complex being erected in the valley.

"What are they going to do when the well runs dry—literally?" Carolyn said.

"Ah, the unintended consequences of overbuilding in an arid climate. Panic? Maybe, it won't. Hopefully, we won't be around to find out."

"Too bad greed always wins," Carolyn concluded.

Kirsten lifted her glass. "Amen to that."

After dinner, Kirsten drove straight to Carolyn's apartment. She parked at the curb. "Your car's still in one piece and the tires have been changed, but I still rather wait for you. It would be safer if we remained together."

"I don't think he'll bother us anymore tonight. Go on home and I'll be there as soon as I grab some clothes. I also need to check my mail and call my lawyer."

"Just don't take too long."

"I won't," Carolyn promised.

Carolyn must have been about a half-hour, but by the time she reached Kirsten's condo, no one answered the door. The lights were on in the kitchen, though. Why would they be on if Kirsten wasn't home? Maybe they were on a timer. That was a possibility. Carolyn began to wonder if her friend had stopped at the supermarket on the way home. Only, wouldn't she have told Carolyn, or left her a key? She had made Carolyn promise not to be too long. No. Something was terribly wrong. Carolyn could feel it in her bones. And she knew James was somehow involved.

If something happened to Kirsten because of Carolyn's poor judgment when it came to me, she'd never forgive herself. She dropped her overnight bag and started to walk around the condo toward the back when she was roughly grabbed. A gloved hand covered her mouth and pulled her backward.

"Hello, sweetheart. I figured I give you a warm welcome," James cooed in her ear. "I'm going to take my hand away. Do not scream or you will be sorry."

"What did you do to Kirsten?" Carolyn spat.

"Come, darling, I'll take you to her," he said, propelling her to the door.

The manner in which James said that made Carolyn sick to her stomach. She stopped abruptly and whirled around to face James. "If you hurt her—"

"You'll do what? Carolyn, don't you realize that you have no leverage here? And you know what, after I'm done here, I'm going to get away scot-free."

"I've already changed my will. You'll not get a penny."

"There are ways to contest wills, but let's not get ahead of ourselves," James replied, roughly shoving her. "Now get going."

***

Carl landed and picked up his car rental. He tapped his sister's address into the GPS. His watch read 8:15. Carolyn would be home from work now. Perhaps he'd finally meet the nemesis, James. Only when he got there an hour later, no one was there. He knocked and rang her bell, even called her landline and cell. None of which was answered. Beads of sweat began to form on his forehead. Where the hell was she? Just before his imagination galloped away with his reasoning, he realized she could be out to dinner. So why hadn't she answered her cell? Noisy restaurant. You've been there, done that. Stop getting distracted by ridiculousness, he reminded himself.

Next, he put Kirsten's address into the GPS, hoping for better results. Then he dialed her cell, but only got her voice mail. Should he stay and wait for Carolyn or go to Kirsten's. She knew he was coming and would most likely be waiting for him. Then he remembered her telling him that if he came too early and she wasn't there to look for a spare key under the yellow flowerpot and let himself in.

***

James prodded and pushed Carolyn into the backdoor of Kirsten's condo. By that time, she was fearing the worst. Her friend was most likely already dead because of her. And the sight that greeted her when she reached the kitchen reinforced her gruesome thoughts.

Kirsten was duck-taped to one of the kitchen chairs, her head lolling to one side.

"You bastard!" Carolyn cried out and pummeled his chest.

James grabbed her fists and said, "Cool, down. She's not dead—yet and then laughed.

"What did you do to her?"

"Just a mild sedative. I want her to be alert for my big finale here."

Carolyn shook her head. "What's wrong with you?"

"Don't you already know? Why else are you divorcing me? I already figured out who the snitch was," he said, pointing to Kirsten. "We were fine until she butted her nose in our business."

"She had nothing to do with my decision to divorce you."

"Stop lying and sit down in that chair!"

Carolyn's heart began to thud in her chest. She knew damn well that this was it for her and Kirsten. She'd go to her grave knowing that everything was entirely her fault. She decided not to make things easy for James. "No."

"Come on, Carolyn, you're only delaying things. Besides, this isn't a democracy. You have no say in the matter."

"And if I refuse to sit down?" she asked, defiantly.

"Then I just kill you now," James said brandishing a large serrated hunting knife.

"Tell me, James, did you ever love me at all? Or was our entire romance and marriage a sham?"

"Nah, that's only part of it. I do enjoy showing you high-class broads with money that a guy like me can win their hearts, but it's the money stupid."

That rebuke stung her. "That's exactly what Kirsten thought. She didn't want me to marry you."

"You should have taken her advice, Carolyn."

Carl found the key under the yellow flowerpot and let himself inside. He heard voices and realized that one was his sister's and she sounded petrified. He took his service revolver from his bag. Being a detective had its perks he always told people. Protection was one of them. Then he silently went into the kitchen. "Put the knife down!" Carl commanded.

At that moment two things occurred. Recognizing the voice, Carolyn broke into a wide smile and felt salvation was at hand and James pivoted on the balls of his feet ready to charge the owner of the voice but thought better of it when he saw the size of Carl holding the gun. "Now put the knife on the floor and kick it toward me."

When James complied, he was ordered to sit down in the chair he'd earlier designated for Carolyn. Carl cuffed James to the chair and then called 911. Then he took his sister in his arms and hugged her tightly.

"Are you all right, Carolyn?"

"I am now, but I need to make certain that Kirsten is too."

Carolyn went to Kirsten and began to cut off her restraints when she began to come out of whatever James had drugged her with. She opened her eyes which were filled with fright but smiled when she saw Carolyn bending over her.

"Do you want some water, Kirsten?" Carolyn asked.

Carl filled a glass with some from the refrigerator and handed it to Kirsten. "Thanks for leaving the key."

"You knew about Carl coming to Arizona? Why didn't you tell me?"

It wasn't Kirsten, but Carl who replied to Carolyn. "I was coming to get you to leave that son-of-a-bitch," he said pointing to Carl, "and feared you might not listen."

"Some things are truly too good to be true, Carolyn," Kirsten said.

"Amen to that, sister," Carl said.

The police arrived at that point and hauled James off. Carolyn felt as if the weight of an albatross was cut from around her neck. She'd learned an important lesson. No more rushing into relationships.

THE END

DISAPPOINTED
By Candace Gold

Scott greeted me at the door with a long-stemmed rose. Instead of finding it romantic, I subconsciously began to subtract its cost from our meager savings account.

When the huge smile on his face turned to disappointment, I forced myself to smile and say, "Thank you, Scott." Secretly hoping that he'd found a job, I asked, "What's the occasion?"

"No special occasion. I merely wanted to celebrate us, Susan."

As Scott helped me off with my jacket, I could smell the unmistakable aroma of Italian food. Having had little more than a bunch of soda crackers all day, my mouth had instinctively begun to water. He had dimmed the lights in the dining area and lit two candles to make our dinner more romantic. But how romantic could I feel when I knew he had probably blown what little extra cash we had on such an extravagance?

Thinking about Scott's frivolous use of our money killed my appetite. He noticed that I wasn't eating much of it. Reaching across the table, he touched my hand. "Is there something wrong with your shrimp?"

"No, no—It's fine."

"Then why aren't you eating? I ordered it special because I knew it was your

favorite."

Because we can't afford it! I sorely wanted to scream at him. Instead, I told him, "I'm just not hungry, Scott, that's all."

After Scott helped me clear the dishes and straighten the kitchen, he said, "It's a beautiful night. Let's take a walk."

"Not tonight, Scott. I'm too tired." Aside from not having the luxury of lying down on a couch in front of a TV all day, I really felt drained.

Without masking his disappointment, he replied, "Maybe some other time, then."

I was glad that he didn't press the issue. I was in no mood to have an argument with him tonight. It didn't take a rocket scientist, though, to figure out what Scott's motives were tonight. He was merely trying to recapture the romance that had slipped from our marriage. Things hadn't been too wonderful lately and we were slowly drifting apart. We never made love anymore. Instead, we merely had sex out of necessity. And even that seemed to be happening more and more infrequently.

Not that I was making any excuses for myself, but it was hard to feel sexy, knowing you had to watch every penny you spent so the rent and utilities could be paid every month. Okay, it wasn't Scott's fault that he lost his job as a computer tech. With the economy taking a nosedive, things were tough, and getting another comparable job in his field was difficult. However, taking another job doing something else in the meantime would be better than sitting home all day wishing and hoping. When my pleas fell on deaf ears, I eventually gave up. Being a nagging wife would probably prove unproductive.

"How about me giving you a massage?" Scott suggested.

I realized where that would lead and agreed to it. I had disappointed him enough already. We'd make love and he'd believe that everything was okay. I had been doing that so long that I practically got it down to an art form. Perhaps he had been, too.

Being the office supervisor in a large collection agency, I had much to deal with every day. That made it easy to get involved with my work and forget about my personal life. As far as my co-workers in the department were concerned, my marriage and home life couldn't be better. I didn't wear my problems on my sleeve like some of the others. Airing one's dirty laundry in public just wasn't my style. Perhaps that's why I had little patience for one of the younger reps whose life was an ongoing soap opera with nearly new chapters aired daily.

I confess that I found Josephine immature and irresponsible. I couldn't understand how she could run around whining to anyone who'd listen about her problems, many of which could have been avoided had she made more prudent decisions. Unfortunately, it seemed that I stood alone in my assessment of Josephine's situation and had to keep it to myself. It was never more obvious than the day June cornered me in the employee lounge. I hadn't even sat down before she related the young rep's latest misadventure.

"You'll never believe what's happened to Josephine now," she said, sounding as if the world had spun off its axis.

I couldn't help rolling my eyes. I was certain that whatever it was, June was overreacting. "Now what?" I asked, less than enthusiastic.

"You sound like you don't even care."

"Of course, I care. It's just that you're making it sound so melodramatic."

"Well, it is. Especially since she's still reeling from Jimmy jilting her two days
before the wedding."

"It's devastating for sure, but look on the bright side. Better now than a divorce
later."

"That's a pretty callous thing to say."

"She seemed to get over it pretty fast and seems to have had a good time in Hawaii without him."

"Why shouldn't she have gone, especially if it made her feel better? It wasn't as if the honeymoon trip hadn't already paid for."

"But she could have cashed in the trip and used the money for more important things."

"Well, she didn't and now she really needs our help."

I resented the fact that every time Josephine screwed up it became our problem.

"Isn't there anything she can do by herself?"

"How can you be so mean-spirited?" June asked, making me feel awful. "I only came to you with this problem because you're her supervisor."

By the time the others heard about this conversation, I was going to sound like the biggest bitch in town. If someone extends me any mercy, it will be because they assumed it was my time of the month.

I sighed. "Okay. So, tell me what's wrong now."

"Josephine is going to be evicted from her apartment."

I shook my head. Why wasn't I surprised? "How many months of rent has she missed?"

"Two. Now the landlord wants to evict her."

I wanted to scream at June that the trip to Hawaii would have paid for those two months and then some. "Well, what do you want me to do? The landlord is in his right."

"We could take up a collection—"

"No. I don't think so."

June was looking at me as if I had two heads. "Why are you being so mean? We've got to help Josephine."

"We just can't pass around a hat every time Josephine needs money. She's got to learn to become more responsible," I replied.

Unfortunately, I found myself talking to an empty room, for June had already walked out. I had a funny feeling she was going over my head to the head of personnel. I had no idea what Marcia Dennis would do, but I was glad the situation was out of my hands. Personally, I couldn't afford to give Josephine any money, especially after Scott's expensive dinner last night. I bet Josephine returned all the shower gifts and used the money on her trip to Hawaii. Getting her the toaster oven I gave her put quite a dent in my household budget that month. How would the girl ever learn to spend money wisely if we continually bailed her out every time she drowned in debt?

I tried to keep my mind on my work and not let Josephine and her problems get to me. Luckily, the office was busy, and the morning flew by. At lunch, I went outside to hide in my car. I didn't want anyone to know that I couldn't afford to have a sandwich.

When I returned from lunch, I found that someone had left an inter-office memo on my desk from Marcia Dennis. A fund and food drive had been set up for Josephine. There'd be a jar in Ms. Dennis's office for anyone wishing to donate. As for the food items, a list was typed up. I noticed four of the items had been circled, probably June's doing. Tears filled my eyes. I could hardly afford those four items for myself.

Not wanting to have to stop and talk to anyone, I rushed out of the office at the end of the day. I put the key in the ignition but realized that I couldn't go home and face Scott at that moment, either. I felt like crying. I watched as a smiling Josephine got into her car, acting as if she didn't have a problem in the world.

It was then that I realized I had begun to feel sorry for myself. Was that how it all started? Was the next step the whining and complaining stage? Perhaps I should take note of Josephine's way to cope with financial problems; wring your hands and accept donations. Let others continually bail you out without having to cut back on your excesses or change your lifestyle.

I realized that there were other couples out there who were experiencing what Scott and I were. How were they dealing with it? Were they feeling sorry for themselves? I knew one thing for certain. I couldn't continue to live from day to day continually worrying about being able to pay my bills.

I saw June coming towards my car. I didn't want her to see that I had been crying, so I started the car and pulled out of the spot. Subconsciously I had turned in the opposite direction heading away from home. A moment later, I made the decision to work part-time at my old job. This would certainly help pay for the groceries and if I'm lucky, a little more.

I drove to the diner. Michael, the owner, was behind the register, keying in a bill when I walked in. He smiled when he noticed me and signaled me to wait.

A minute later, he was finished and called Connie, his wife, to take over. She hugged me hello. "You've lost a great deal of weight. Have you been sick?"

"No."

"Where have you been?" Michael asked.

"Things have been tight. Scott's out of work. Can you use me part-time?"

"Of course," he replied, no questions asked. "With every family working two or more jobs, nobody has time to cook anymore. When do you want to start?"

I set up a tentative schedule over some coffee. Now that I was taking charge and doing something positive, I felt better. I realized that it was getting late and headed home

Scott was all over me when I walked through the door. "Where were you? Have you any idea what time it is? Why didn't you call?"

"Can I take my coat off first before you give me the third degree?"

"Well, it's nearly seven-thirty. You had me worried to death. I nearly burned the soup."

The thought of having soup again didn't thrill me. It only made me feel better about stopping at the diner tonight. Soon we'd be able to have decent meals again.

"So, where were you?"

"I stopped to talk to Michael about working at the diner a few nights a week."

"Well, that certainly will make us look terrific. You working two jobs and me—"

Scott threw the spoon he'd been mixing the soup with across the room. It hit the wall and fell down with a clatter. He collapsed in a chair and covered his head with his hands. I put my hand on his shoulder, but he shrugged it off.

"It doesn't have to be like that?"

"And how should it be? How could you even still care for me, Susan? I'm nothing more than a failure."

"No, you're not. Losing your job wasn't your fault. But you've seemed to have given up."

Scott lifted his head to face me. Tears clung to his long, dark lashes. I knew he

was listening and maybe he'd hear what I had to say this time, so I continued.

"It doesn't matter what type of job you're doing right now nor does it have to bring in tons of money. Every little bit helps. Eventually, the economy will get better and you'll be able to get a good job in computers again."

"Yeah, when? Before or after we're too old to have kids?"

My entire world stopped spinning when he said that. Did he just say what I thought he did? Were we going to forget about having a kid once more especially after the promise he'd made to me the last time? I couldn't bear it. Not again.

There was nothing that I wanted more than to have a child. My parents had me late in life and though they were good parents, there were things they couldn't do with me because they were too old. I didn't want this to happen with my children. I also wanted to have more than one.

It seemed that circumstances had caused us to continually put starting a family on hold. First Scott's father got very sick and his medical insurance didn't cover the expenses, so we helped pay the bills. Then his brother needed financial help. After that, we had to save and buy a place to live. It was always something. However, Scott promised on my next birthday in November, no matter what, we'd try to make a baby. I realized that if I allowed his not having a good job get in the way, we'd never have a family because we'd never start. There'd always be something in the way. But, not this time. *Please!*

Yet, I was afraid to ask him what he meant. I'd rather pretend that I never heard him and act as if everything was okay. That way I could still go on believing that when November came I'd throw away my birth control pills.

"I really don't mind working at the diner again," I said bringing us back to what we'd been talking about. And then Scott said something which truly surprised me.

"When I went to Arturo's yesterday, I saw a help-wanted sign in the window of

Computers R Us. Maybe I should go in and check it out."

"That's a great idea."

"You won't have to work at the diner then."

"I think I should, anyway. Whatever extra money I make will help," I said with my goal to start a family in mind. "I'm kind of tired. Can we talk about this tomorrow?"

Though I could tell he was still far from happy about my still wanting to work at the diner, he agreed. I guess he didn't want to argue any more than I did.

"Okay, then. I'm going to wash up and go to bed. I have to get up soon."

I knew that Scott's ego had been badly bruised through all this. That's probably why he couldn't bring himself to work at Computers R Us before I shamed him into it by taking a second job. That hadn't been my intention, but that's how he interpreted my actions. As much as I loved Scott, I seemed to be pushing him away.

As I washed my face, my tears silently slid down my face and slipped into the sink.

My mother often warned me that even a good marriage had its ups and downs. What about the disasters, Mom? What did they have?

Scott's face appeared behind me in the bathroom mirror. "You've got to understand, I don't know how many corporations I've been to looking for a job…"

"I know."

"But, without a good-paying job, how could we afford the baby you want?"

No, Scott, no! Don't tell me we have to postpone starting our family again. We've been married over seven years now and I can feel my biological clock winding down. "Can we talk tomorrow? I'm really exhausted," I said trying to avoid the inevitable.

"I guess," Scott replied and walked out of the bathroom.

I followed him out and we both got into bed, each remaining on our own side,

never touching. I wondered what I was going to do to breach the widening gap between us.

The following morning, I stopped into the employee's lounge to grab a quick cup of coffee. Josephine came waltzing in as if she was on her way to a ball, giggling as if she hadn't a single worry.

"Susan, what do you think of my new dress?" she asked, whirling around in order to model it for me.

Her words exploded in my ears rendering me speechless. How could she afford to go out and buy a new dress when she wasn't able to pay her rent? I never did get a chance to say anything, because June and Theresa walked in. Josephine modeled her new dress for them. Now having a more complete audience, she said, "I sounded so miserable when my dad called yesterday, that he told me to go out and buy myself something nice."

Did he offer to pay for it? I thought to myself.

As if she could read my mind, Josephine giggled and said, "I rushed right out and went shopping. Plastic always comes in handy. And you know what?"

"What?" asked June.

"He was right. I feel so much better now."

Just hearing that made me want to scream. I grabbed my cup of coffee and walked out. As I reached the door I thought I heard Josephine say, "Gee, I wonder what's wrong with her this morning?" All the way back to my office I kept thinking, what was Josephine going to do when the credit card bill came in next month?

Involved in my work, I was able to forget about Josephine for a while. Lunchtime, I took my purse and went out to the car. I had very little to eat for lunch that day, for I was down to the last bit of crackers and the jelly was already gone. I looked forward to getting paid tomorrow and being able to grocery shop.

I had my nose in a book munching on a cracker when someone knocked on my window. I nearly jumped out of my skin. It was Josephine. I rolled down the window.

"We were looking all over for you. Why are you out here?"

"Just needed to get away."

The look on her face told me that she didn't believe my excuse. I noticed that she had her purse and keys with her. She was probably going out for lunch. Thanks to her fellow workers, she could sure do that a great deal. Perhaps they're already feeding the jar with next week's proceeds.

"A few of us are going out for lunch and would like to know if you want to come?"

"Thanks, but I already had lunch."

"Crackers?"

"No. I had a sandwich before. I was still hungry, so I had some crackers."

"Well, if you're still hungry, come with us."

"The crackers did the trick," I replied, feeling stupid that I had to lie.

"Why don't you come anyway? It will be fun—all of us together."

"No. I have a ton of things to do."

"When did you become so serious?" she asked and walked towards her car.

After putting in a full day at the office, I was already tired by the time I got to the diner. By the time I got home, my feet may have been burning and my back aching, but the money in my purse from the tips I'd gotten made it all worth it. And this was only a

weekday night. That meant the weekend had to be even better.

I found Scott dozing in front of the TV. I guess he had tried to wait up for me. I

took the remote and shut off the TV. He waked and yawned. "What time is it Susan?"

"It's really late and I'm tired."

"I was waiting up for you..."

"You didn't have to, but thanks." I wanted to apologize for the argument we had last night, but the words wouldn't come out.

"How was the diner?"

"Pretty busy for a weekday. I'm looking forward to the weekend."

"Really? How did you do in tips?"

"Fifty-seven dollars."

"Wow! That sure beats seven-twenty an hour."

"You got the job at Computers R Us?"

"Yeah. I start tomorrow."

"That's great."

"Now that I got a job, you won't have to work two."

"I don't mind, Scott."

"You can't tell me you're not exhausted and your feet aren't killing you."

"I won't lie. What you say is true, but I'll feel better with the extra money."

"Well, *I* won't."

"Why? It can only help. Just think I can go food shopping before work tomorrow morning and get some real food for a change. When was the last time you had a cold beer with dinner?"

Scott sighed. "Let me do the shopping tomorrow since I start work later than you

do."

I agreed and went straight to bed. I was so exhausted that I fell asleep the minute

my head hit the pillow despite the fact I knew there was a great deal left unsaid between Scott and me, fearing I'd increased the gap growing between us just a little more.

The following morning I woke up with a terrible headache. I practically dragged myself to work. I couldn't but help think about Scott and what he said and didn't say

last night and the night before. We had been avoiding talking things out like we used to, skirting around the major issues. I know he didn't want to hurt me and tell me what was so obvious. And I tried to keep him from telling me exactly that. But I couldn't bear to wait any longer. I was going to be thirty-one on my next birthday. True, it wasn't old, but... but what if it didn't turn out to be easy? What if it was going to take a while? I wanted us to become a family. I didn't think we'd ever be rich and live in the lap of luxury. But, we'd have each other. We certainly didn't have much now. I loved Scott with all my heart and yet I could feel him slipping away along with my dreams.

"Are you okay, Susan?" Josephine asked, interrupting my thoughts.

"Sorry, I didn't hear you come in."

"What's wrong? I mean, do you want to talk about it? It'll help."

A tear dripped onto my hand. It was then I realized I'd been crying. I felt somewhat embarrassed since Josephine was probably the last person in the world I'd cry my heart out to.

"Nothing's wrong. Everything's fine."

"You sure don't look like it is."

"No, it is. Was there something you wanted?"

"Oh, yes. I need your signature on this," she said, handing me a release form.

"If you need to talk, I'm right outside."

Forcing myself to smile, I thanked her. She was right about one thing, though. I

should talk about what was bothering me. Only the person I should speak to was Scott.

Even if it meant shattering my dream.

The smell of sizzling meat delighted my senses as I walked into our home that night. I worked a few hours at the diner but promised to have dinner with Scott when I got home. He had broiled hamburgers and fries. Boy, did they smell good.

As he placed the food on the table, we made some small talk. He seemed to be in a better mood. And he seemed to like his new job despite the fact it didn't pay very well.

He opened two cold bottles of beer into frosty glasses. "You don't know how long I waited for this," he said.

I smiled. It had been one of the luxuries we had crossed off our grocery list when he lost his job. "You can have mine. I'm really not in the mood."

"Gee, that's too bad. I like the way you get when you drink a little."

"Hmm, was that why you bought the stuff? To have your way with me?"

"Maybe. We can both use a little loosening up. Things have been pretty slow in that department recently."

"You're right. We haven't been very close these past months."

"I want things to be the way they were. I know they would be if I hadn't lost my job. I wanted us to be able to have a baby as we planned. I know I promised..."

"Oh, Scott, please don't tell me I have to wait again," I pleaded with him. Tears filled my eyes quickly and threatened to fall.

"Hey, watch it!" he said pushing my beer away from me. There's no reason to cry in your beer."

I looked at him. How could he be worried about beer when he was about to take away the one thing I wanted?

"We lost sight of our dreams, didn't we? We were always there for others who needed our help, but we weren't exactly there for each other. I was nursing a hurt ego and you the fear of not having a baby before we ran out of time."

Well, it was all out in the open now. Scott reached across the table and took my hand in his. I guess he wanted to be as gentle as possible.

"I made a promise and I aim to keep it. We'll find a way to make our bills after the baby is born. I guess sometimes you have to have a little faith."

I couldn't believe it. He wasn't going to break his promise, after all! No matter what, Scott and I were going to have a family. My tears were streaming down my face now.

"It's a good thing I moved your beer. We wouldn't want to ruin it. After all, you've got some making up to do."

I laughed when he said that. "I don't need a beer to make love to my husband."

For the first time in months, Scott and I made love that night. It felt wonderful.

And as we snuggled afterward, I realized that life was indeed a bunch of choices. I always tried to make the right ones. But, no matter what, I'd never become like Josephine and depend on others to bail me out. Now that I knew that Scott would allow me to have my special birthday present, I realized that I'd be able to wait a short time if necessity warranted it. After all, I couldn't let my selfish desire for children force me to make a poor decision. The very fact that I no longer had to pretend, and things were back on track between Scott and me made everything truly wonderful. We had each other and with God's help, maybe a baby soon, to share our love with.

The End

Other Titles by Candace Gold

The Twist of Fate
The Promise
A Heated Romance
Crazy Love
Reverie
And Justice for All
I Confess
The Greatest Gift of All
Raped by the Law
Return to Hell
I was Stalked by my Own Man
Under a Kinder Moon
Twisted Love
Summer Rain
Left to Die
Candace Gold's Book Shorts

ABOUT THE AUTHOR

With over 200 short stories, numerous anthologies, 35 novellas and novels in print, whether she's writing less edgy contemporary romance, or spicy hot erotica as Candy Caine, she keeps her husband, Robert, on his toes in their Arizona home. Supportive with her writing career, he's always willing to help her add authenticity to the scenes in her stories. After all, technique is so important for good writing. Her biggest thrill is to bring the joy of reading to others.